Mrs. Griffin is Missing
and other stories

Mrs. Griffin is Missing
and other stories

Anna Christian

iUniverse, Inc.
New York Lincoln Shanghai

Mrs. Griffin is Missing and other stories

iUniverse books may be ordered through booksellers or by contacting:

iUniverse
2021 Pine Lake Road, Suite 100
Lincoln, NE 68512
www.iuniverse.com
1-800-Authors (1-800-288-4677)

ISBN-13: 978-0-595-37041-2 (pbk)
ISBN-13: 978-0-595-81445-9 (ebk)
ISBN-10: 0-595-37041-1 (pbk)
ISBN-10: 0-595-81445-X (ebk)

Printed in the United States of America

This book is dedicated to Junior, Big Sis, Bobby, and MJ

Contents

Preface

*H*arlem of the 1950's was very different than it is today. Six story tenements flanked most streets. Each block was like a tiny village. Along the blocks were small stores that catered to the community needs. It was not unusual to have a grocery story, laundry, church, or candy store interspersed among the buildings. Residents on the block knew each other, if not personally, than by sight. During the summers, the streets teemed with activity. People perched in windows to gaze down at the goings-on below or to catch whatever breezes flowed through these canyons of concrete. Often neighborhood men sat along the sidewalk playing checkers on makeshift tables, while older women rested on kitchen chairs blocking the entranceways to their buildings, exchanging the latest gossip and keeping watch over the children who played in the street. Depending upon the season, children organized various games. In the winter, they skated or built sleds and raced down the slight hills like the one that ran from 144th street to 145th. Spring was kite-flying season; summer was the time for stoopball and stickball. Going downtown meant going to 125th street to shop for clothes, to dine in a fine restaurant like the Baby Grand, or to watch well-known entertainers perform at the Apollo Theater. In the 1960's, though, projects, rising like giants towering over the community, began to replace many of the six story tenements built half a century before. As the population increased, the sense of community faded. The following stories take place during the comparatively innocuous time of the 1950's.

The Secret in Apartment 2C

Chapter One

*T*ap, tap, tap!

Startled, Bobby Thompson looked up from his math homework to where the sound was coming from, but it stopped before he could fix the location. He listened for a moment. The third floor apartment was quiet. No sounds other than the street traffic and the clock ticking on the wall penetrated the silence. He began to work again.

Tap, tap, tap!

There it was again. It was coming from the pipe near the radiator. This was the third time in two weeks that Bobby had heard it. Throwing down his pencil and closing his books, he raced over to listen. It came from the apartment below. In a flash, he ran down to Apartment 2C and knocked on the door. No one answered. Just like before. He knocked again. Still no answer. After standing there for several minutes, he gave up and went back upstairs. "Somebody was knocking again today," Bobby said that evening as the family sat down to dinner.

"Did you go downstairs and ask them to stop?" Mrs. Thompson asked.

"I knocked on the door a lot of times, but nobody answered."

"Of course nobody would answer. Because nobody's home. Miss Henderson works all day."

"You sure you heard knocking? You sure it wasn't your imagination?" Brenda asked.

He frowned at her. At thirteen, Brenda's chief interests were clothes, boys, and making Bobby angry. With large brown eyes, thick braids down to her shoulders, and a very pretty face that was sometimes overlooked because of her chubby body, Brenda looked just like her mother except she lacked her mother's energy. Nothing satisfied her more than to spend most of the day in bed reading Harlequin romances and watching TV soaps.

"That's strange," said Mr. Thompson. "You seem to be the only one who hears these noises."

He was a tall, well-built man with a receding hairline, a bushy mustache, and two deep dimples that showed even when he was not smiling which wasn't often. His work as a postman kept him in good shape physically except for the beginning of a potbelly.

Bobby felt his stomach muscles tighten beneath his tee shirt. He glared at his parents and sister as they plunged into their food as if they hadn't eaten in a week.

"Every time I tell you about something, you never believe me," he cried, his voice rising. If he wasn't so hungry, he'd get up and leave.

"They don't mean anything by it," said Mrs. Thompson. "Now you all don't go teasing him. Eat your dinner, son." A petite woman, with short, uneven limp hair because of too much pressing, and a honey brown complexion, she worked as a beautician at Sarah's House of Style located on Amsterdam Avenue. Sometimes after standing on her feet all day doing hair, she would turn rope with Brenda and her friends as they jumped Double Dutch.

"How come it only happens when you're here by yourself?" asked Brenda.

"Maybe if one of us heard it, we might believe you. But you've got to admit, you got a wild imagination. Remember when you told us you saw…"

Bobby didn't hear the rest of what his father was saying. He leaped from the table and ran to his room. He lay across the bed with his arms tucked behind his head staring up at the ceiling.

"They don't believe me," he thought. "They ain't never gonna believe me until I can prove it."

Chapter Two

"You got to come home with me," Bobby pleaded with his friend Bubba as they walked home from school the next day. "Just for a couple of minutes. I need a witness."

"For what?" Bubba kicked a can into the gutter. Like Bobby, he was eleven years old, but unlike Bobby, Bubba was big for his age. He loved to eat and it showed.

One of the reasons they were best friends was because they were so much alike except Bubba wore glasses and his hair was cut so short it looked as if it was painted on his head. Bobby's hair was thick and matted and whenever his mother didn't catch him and make him comb it, it would be filled with lint from his pillow.

"You got to come because if you hear any knocking, you can tell my folks. Then, they'll believe me."

As they passed Bubba's building, Bobby grabbed his arm and pulled him along. Bubba resisted.

"I don't feel like it. Besides, the guys are playing stick ball, and as soon as I finish eating, I'm gonna see if they'll let me play." Bubba sat down to tie his sneaker on one of the garbage cans that stood near the curb. "What makes you think it ain't Miss Henderson?"

"Because she usually be working till evening. Ain't nobody home. That's what makes it so weird." Bobby's voice rose with excitement. His hands moved wildly as if to convince Bubba. "You got to come home with me."

"I can't, man," Bubba said starting up the steps to his building. "Maybe tomorrow."

Bobby watched him disappear into the dark hallway. Then, with his head down and his shoulders slumped, he started for his apartment building three doors away. As he passed the second floor landing, he glanced over at Apartment 2C. On tiptoe, he moved towards the steel frame and pressed his ear against the cold metal.

"And just what do you think you're doing?"

He jumped. Turning and peering into the shadows of the dimly lit hallway, he saw a broad figure coming towards him. It was Charlotte Henderson. Standing over five feet seven, she looked like a giant next to Bobby who was barely four feet nine.

Charlotte worked odd hours as a nurse's aide at Harlem Hospital. She'd lived in the same apartment most of her life taking care of her invalid mother.

When she was young, Charlotte rarely left her apartment, and when she did, she seldom spoke to anyone. The children on the block called her names. After her mother died, Charlotte disappeared. This caused a brief stir in the neighborhood. Then she was quickly forgotten. No one knew where she'd gone and few cared. Then suddenly, after a twelve-year absence, she had returned. Now she lived in the apartment she had grown up in, as silent and alone as before.

"Why have you got your ear pressed against my door?" she asked, her voice vibrating with anger.

"I was trying to see if anybody was home," he stammered. He felt his heart beating fast. "Well, why didn't you just knock instead of acting like a thief. What do you want anyway?"

"I…uh…I thought I heard somebody inside. I thought maybe it was a robber and…" his mind went blank. Backing towards the steps, he almost stumbled. Quickly recovering his balance, he fled up the steps to his apartment.

Chapter Three

"*H*ear any more strange noises today?" teased Brenda as they washed the dinner dishes. Before he could answer, his mother broke in.

"Leave him alone," she said putting the leftovers into the refrigerator. "Bobby, when you finish drying the dishes, I want you to take the garbage out."

"And watch out for ghosts," Brenda added, ducking just in time to miss the towel Bobby threw at her.

He grumbled to himself as he gathered the bags of garbage and pulled them out into the hall. How he hated this chore. Of all his chores, this one always filled him with dread. Stray cats and dogs hung around the cans, but they didn't bother him as much as the rats. Several times he'd seen them foraging about the garbage for food. Whenever he saw them, he remembered the neighbor's small son who had been bitten last year.

He sped down the three flights of stairs and out to the backyard where Mr. Brown, the super, kept the large cans. As he dumped the garbage into them, he noticed a light in the Henderson's kitchen window. Overwhelmed with curiosity, he climbed onto the fire escape and crept to her window. A thick shade blocked his view but when he lay down on his stomach, he could just barely see inside. It looked as if Charlotte was talking to someone, or could it be the TV? He wasn't sure. Then, he saw the silhouette of someone against the shade. Whoever it was was small. Much shorter than Charlotte.

'It can't be a visitor?' he thought. 'I ain't never seen nobody except Charlotte go in or out of there before.'

He crouched down for a better look. Suddenly the clang of a garbage can top hitting the concrete sent cats howling and scurrying in all directions. Startled, Bobby jumped up so quickly, he almost fell off the fire escape. Still shaking from the noise, he hurriedly made his way through the now darkened yard to the inside of his building, not stopping until he was safely inside his apartment.

When several days passed without any unusual noises, Bobby forgot about the incident. A week went by and all was quiet whenever he was home alone. Then, the day before the school term ended, the knocking started again.

This time Bobby tiptoed to the back window and stepped out onto the fire escape. He ran down to the window below and pressed his face against the pane.

A thin curtain blocked his view. Noticing that the window was open about an inch from the bottom, he decided to take a chance. Slowly, he stuck his hands under the frame and began to raise it as quietly as he could.

"Hey! What are you doing up there?" Bobby looked down. There below him was Mr. Brown, the super, who was seldom seen except in the wee hours of the morning hauling garbage cans to the sidewalk for collection. A skinny, unshaven man, Brown looked like a scarecrow in his worn clothes and dirty brown hat.

Bobby lost no time stumbling up to his apartment.

"Bobby Thompson? I know it's you!" Mr. Brown yelled after him. "I'm gonna tell your father when I see him! You should be ashamed of yourself!"

He shook his fist up at the window. Then turning his back, he started across the yard in his slow dragging way. Bobby watched from behind the curtain as Mr. Brown disappeared between the buildings.

Chapter Four

"*B*obby, you been around the Henderson apartment again? This is the last time I'm gonna tell you," Mr. Thompson said the next morning as he got ready for work. "Next time I hear about you going near that place, you're gonna be sorry."

"But Dad, Charlotte don't live there alone. There's somebody else…"

"It's Miss Henderson to you, and it's none of our business who lives with her. You got no right to spy on people. She don't bother us, and we're not gonna bother her. You understand?"

"How come we never see nobody going in or out except Miss Henderson? Don't she have any friends?" Bobby asked, missing the frown on his father's face. "She must be hiding somebody that she don't want us to know about, like that movie we saw on TV the other night. These people only let this man out at night and…"

"I'm not gonna tell you no more. Leave her alone!" Mr. Thompson said, firmly closing the subject or so he thought.

From that moment on, though, Bobby was determined to find out who else lived in Apartment 2C. With the school term finally over, he could devote more time to solving this mystery. He tried to get Bubba to help but he was leaving for his grandparents' farm in North Carolina and wouldn't be back until the end of August. Bobby would have to find out on his own.

Early Monday morning, after everyone had gone, he crept down the fire escape once more. As before, the window was slightly opened. A breeze fluttered the curtains. After checking the yard below to make sure no one was watching, he raised the window as quietly as he could and climbed inside. For a second, his father's warning flashed across his mind, but as always, his curiosity was much stronger than his fears. Slowly, he glanced around the kitchen. The door leading to the other rooms was closed. He listened for a moment before pushing it open. In one room, he saw a large bed in the corner with a crocheted cover thrown over the end. He knew it was Charlotte's room because of the perfume that seemed to linger in the air and the several pairs of white shoes that stood in front of the closet just below the nurses' uniforms hanging just inside.

Cautiously, he crept to the living room and looked around. The whole place had a bare look to it. At least it did to him. His home was neat but filled with years of living. As much as she tried to get rid of clutter, Mrs. Thompson fought an uphill battle. Mr. Thompson loved to collect odds and ends, some valuable, some not. Brenda was always making doll clothes and needed scraps of material. Bobby, too, was a pack rat. He saved every comic book, baseball cards for trading, and every toy he'd ever received. Mrs. Thompson loved to read and whenever she'd pass a secondhand bookstore, she seldom emerged without purchasing several.

As Bobby started back to the kitchen, he heard music coming from behind the door of one of the rooms he hadn't looked into. It was turned so low he almost missed it.

Getting down on his knees, he approached the door and pushed it open slowly. There, sitting at the desk with his back to the door was a boy. Clad in bathrobe and pajamas, he looked to be the same age as Bobby, yet he was so thin and frail looking. Without thinking, Bobby stood up, knocking over a nearby chair.

"Is that you, Mama?" The boy turned and when Bobby saw his wandering gaze, he knew that the boy was blind.

"I'm sorry," Bobby said suddenly feeling very guilty. "I live upstairs and…"

The boy dropped what he was holding and moved quickly to the far corner of the room and to the floor. His arms covered his face as if to ward off an attack; he began to hyperventilate. Bobby had seen a student in his class do the same thing. His teacher had given the girl a paper bag and told her to breathe into it.

"I ain't gonna hurt you," Bobby said, moving towards the boy. But as his breathing grew louder, harsher, Bobby backed away.

"I'm going. I'm sorry. I didn't mean to scare you." Feeling helpless, he turned and quickly left the apartment.

All that evening Bobby waited for some sign that his parents knew that he had entered the Henderson's apartment against their orders. He wanted to tell them about the boy but he didn't dare. Fortunately the evening passed as usual.

Several days later, while Bobby was watching his favorite cartoon on TV, he heard a tap on the pipe again. This time he tapped back. It was soon followed by yet another tap. Bobby responded. While he wanted to see the boy again, he didn't want to frighten him. The image of the boy crouched in the corner crying kept Bobby from repeating his earlier actions. Soon, what started out simply as an acknowledgment of each other's presence developed into a code, a signal. Each day Bobby looked forward to being alone so he could communicate with the boy.

*   *   *   *

One day, when the boy tapped, Bobby decided to take a chance. Armed with a sandwich his mother left him for lunch, he ran down to Apartment 2C and tapped out their signal on the door. After several minutes, it opened slowly and the boy stood beside it, a frightened look on his face.

"Hi, my name's Bobby and I brought you a sandwich." Bobby reached over and placed the sandwich in the boy's hand. "I hope you like tuna. It's my favorite," he said.

The boy took the sandwich and moved carefully towards the kitchen. Bobby stood in the doorway watching him. Before he reached the kitchen, the boy turned.

"You can come in for a while if you want," he said softly. Bobby sat down at the table, fascinated as he watched the boy move around the kitchen unaided, taking two glasses and plates from the cupboard, milk from the refrigerator, and filling the two glasses. When he was done, he sat down beside Bobby.

"You move around real good for a blind guy."

The boy said nothing. He gave Bobby one-half of the sandwich while he ate the other.

"Do you like it?" Bobby asked. "My mother made it this morning."

The boy nodded. When they had finished eating, the boy took the dishes to the sink and washed them. Bobby reached for a towel to dry, but the boy waved him off.

"What's your name?" Bobby asked when the boy sat down again. The boy drew in a deep breath as if he had to gather his strength to talk.

"Sonny," he said. It was so low Bobby had to lean forward to hear.

After a long awkward moment of silence, Bobby began to feel nervous. He shifted in his chair so violently it fell over sending him crashing to the floor. Sonny jumped and would have fled from the room if Bobby had not started laughing. Getting up off the floor, he described what had happened.

Sonny threw back his head and laughed, too. The strain broken, Bobby told Sonny about his attempts to discover who was tapping on the pipes. Sonny explained that soon after he and his mother moved in, he discovered that his room was right beneath Bobby's.

"Sometimes, at night, I'd hear you arguing with your sister and I'd wish I had a brother or sister."

"You can have mine any day."

"That day you suddenly showed up, I got scared."

"It scared me too. I'm sorry I snuck in on you. How come I never see you playing outside?"

When Sonny didn't answer, Bobby quickly changed the subject.

"Do you like music? I heard you playing some the day I came down."

Almost immediately a smile spread across Sonny's face. He jumped up from the table and, motioning Bobby to follow, he led him to his room. It was a small room, just like Bobby's except that in the corner, over the desk was the largest collection of records, tapes and albums Bobby had ever seen.

"Is all this yours? Musta cost a lot of money."

Sonny selected a record and put it on an expensive-looking turntable. Instantly the room was flooded with music. For hours they sang, beat out rhythms, and had a fine time. Bobby even danced a little. Before the day was over, Bobby looked at Sonny with new admiration. Sonny knew more about music and musicians than Bobby thought possible. He knew a little about blues, jazz, rhythm and blues, rock, gospel and even some classical. It was like being in school except this was fun. Sonny told Bobby about Charlie Parker and John Coltrane, Leadbelly, and Bessie Smith, the Orioles, the Soul Stirrers, and Chopin.

"How did you learn all that stuff?" Bobby asked.

"My mother teaches me. What she doesn't know, she gets books and reads to me."

At four o'clock, Sonny turned the music off.

"My mother'll be home any minute now, and I'm not suppose to have anybody in here," he explained as he led Bobby to the door.

Just as they reached it, they heard the sound of someone fumbling for keys.

"I better go out the back way," Bobby whispered, hurrying towards the kitchen. "I'll come back tomorrow, if you want."

He barely made it through the window before the door opened and Charlotte walked in carrying a bag of groceries. For a moment he watched from outside as she emptied the bag and put the groceries away. Then he turned and ran upstairs.

Chapter Five

Bobby and Sonny became good friends that summer. During the day when no one was at home, Bobby went down to Sonny's apartment, and they would spend hours listening to music, playing checkers which Sonny would always win, and making up stories based on the comic books Bobby brought with him. Bobby did not tell his parents about their friendship for fear they would be angry with him for disobeying their orders. Once in a while Brenda would try to tease him about hearing noises, but Bobby would let it pass.

After several weeks of meeting in secret, Bobby suggested they go outside.

"Let's go over to the park and hear these guys playing congas," he said eagerly.

At the mention of going outside, Sonny's body stiffened and his voice grew tense.

"I think Art Tatum was the greatest jazz piano player that ever lived. My mother said he could pack a thousand notes in one measure."

"You gotta hear these congas players. They're really bad. They get together almost every day and play for hours. And anybody can jump in if they want to."

"Let me put on this record. I bet you never heard anything like it before." Sonny placed another record on the turntable without giving it the meticulous cleaning he usually did.

"Don't you want to go out? It's a great day, not too hot yet."

"I hate it outside," Sonny said, finally. "It's so dirty and too many people and…cars everywhere."

"Aw, common. It'll be fun."

"I can't," Sonny replied suddenly growing very quiet.

"But why can't you? You ain't scared, are you?"

"I said I don't want to!" Sonny flung down the 78'phonograph record* he was holding and it shattered into pieces on the floor.

Bobby decided, for the moment, that it was best to let the matter drop. However, as the days sped by, Bobby's restlessness grew. While he liked being with Sonny, seeing the other children playing in the street outside Sonny's window, filled him with longing. He wished he could join them. He began to cut his visits short. Instead of staying until just before Charlotte returned from work, he'd leave at three o'clock, then two o'clock. One day he left at noon. Each time he left, he noticed the hurt look on Sonny's face, but his friend never said anything.

*   *   *   *

Whenever he'd leave Sonny's apartment, Bobby would wander through the hot Harlem streets and watch the other kids play stoopball. Sometimes he'd join them, or he'd catch the double feature at the Odeon. Occasionally he'd go swimming at Colonial pool along with Freddie, one of his classmates who, like him, was trapped in the city during the summer. Bobby didn't care much for him because all Freddie talked about was fighting and girls. Still, it was better than being by himself.

One day, when Bobby went down to see Sonny, he was met with a surprise.

"I'm ready to go," Sonny said as soon as he opened the door to let Bobby in. "If you take me to the store, I'll treat you to some ice cream."

Sonny gripped Bobby's arm as they approached the stairs and began going down. The closer they got to the street, however, the tighter Sonny held Bobby's arm, so tight that Bobby could feel the boy's body tremble beside him. Three women blocking the entranceway shifted a bit to let them pass.

---

* *78 RPM were phonograph records up until the mid 1950's. They were easily breakable.*

"Who's your friend, Bobby?" Mrs. Mobley called out as he maneuvered Sonny around their chairs. The neighborhood gossips would have a lot to talk about that day, Bobby thought.

"His name's Sonny," was all Bobby replied as he quickened his steps, pulling Sonny behind him.

"Those women sit out on the stoop all day and get into everybody's business," Bobby explained when they were out of hearing distance.

"It's even hotter out here than it was upstairs," Bobby said with a laugh. "You sure you want to go to the store?"

Sonny said nothing.

Sweat poured from Sonny's brow as he walked haltingly beside Bobby. No sooner did they reach the corner when suddenly Sonny dropped to the sidewalk in a faint. Bobby's heart began to race as a crowd quickly formed around them. Before Bobby could think, he heard someone in the crowd cry out.

"What have you done to my child?" To Bobby's surprise, Charlotte was there. Having gotten off from work early, she'd done some grocery shopping and was looking forward to making Sonny's favorite dessert, apple cake. The memory of what had happened to her son just a few years before came flooding back. She trembled with rage. Lifting Sonny's thin body in her great arms, she carried him into the building and up to their apartment. Bobby trailed behind carrying the packages she had dropped.

"Get me a wet towel!" she yelled. By the time Bobby dashed into the bathroom and brought back the towel, Sonny had come around.

"What was he doing out in the street?" she demanded, her voice sending chills down Bobby's spine.

"We was just going to the store for some ice cream," he managed to squeak.

"Ice cream!" she screamed. "You took him in the street to buy ice cream? Get out of my house and don't you ever come back!"

Bobby didn't hesitate. He ran as fast as he could out of Apartment 2C and upstairs to his home.

Chapter Six

That evening as the Thompsons sat down to dinner, they were startled by a knock on the door. Brenda ran to answer it.

"It's that woman from downstairs," she whispered. "She wants to talk to Daddy, probably about Bobby."

Mr. Thompson wiped his mouth with his napkin and started for the living room.

"You stay here," he said to Bobby who was about to follow. As Bobby watched the door close behind him, his appetite suddenly disappeared.

"What have you been up to now?" Mrs. Thompson said noting that Bobby's normally animated face had grown increasingly somber as if he were in pain.

"I bet I know what he's been doing," said Brenda. "My girlfriend Paula said she been seeing him go in and out of Miss Henderson's apartment for weeks now."

"What have you been going into that woman's apartment for?" said Mrs. Thompson, her voice rising.

"Didn't your daddy and I tell you to stay away from there?"

Before he could answer, Mr. Thompson returned, anger pulling in his dimples even more than when he smiled. Bobby looked up at his father, his eyes sparkling with tears.

"Boy, you better have a good explanation for this!"

* * * *

"What's the boy's name again?" Mrs. Thompson asked later that evening.

"Sonny," answered Bobby. Now that everything was out in the open, he felt much better. Still, the result of Charlotte's meeting with his father was that he couldn't visit Sonny anymore. He made a promise to his parents and this time he intended to keep it even though he'd miss Sonny.

"You can't blame Miss Henderson for wanting to protect him," Mrs. Thompson went on. "Children can be so cruel to one another." She shook her head. Mr. Thompson put down his paper and looked over at Bobby.

"I know you would never do anything to harm Sonny like those other boys did. But we've got to respect Miss Henderson's wishes."

"Did they really push him into the street?" Brenda asked.

"They didn't push him. She said these boys took him out to the middle of the street and left him there. He got hit by a car. That's why she doesn't trust anybody with him but herself."

*   *   *   *

The news of Sonny's presence quickly spread around the neighborhood. After a while, though, it died a natural death. Because nobody saw him since he fainted on the sidewalk, and because Charlotte Henderson talked to no one, everybody soon forgot that she had a son, and things returned to normal; for all except Bobby, that is. Although he tapped on the pipes daily, it drew no response from Sonny.

Chapter Seven

*T*ap! tap! tap! tap!…tap! tap! tap! tap!

Bobby was startled when he heard Sonny beating frantically on the pipes and calling his name. He raced down to Apartment 2C and knocked on the door. Sonny was highly agitated. When he had calmed down, he told Bobby that Charlotte had been in an accident and was in the hospital."

"I want to see my mother. Can you take me to see her?"

"Who told you she was in the hospital?"

"A nurse who works with my mother stopped by to tell me. She asked if I had anyone to stay with me and I told her I could stay with your family, if it's all right. Can we go now, please?"

"Even if we did get there, we won't be able to get in," Bobby responded. "Not without grownups with us. And even then, they won't let us to go upstairs to the rooms."

Bobby had been to Harlem Hospital once when his grandmother was there. He hadn't been allowed to go up to see her. Instead he had to wait in the lobby for his parents to return. Nevertheless, when Sonny insisted, he promised to take him. It wasn't until they were almost to the street that Bobby remembered what had happened the last time they went out.

"You sure you can make it? You ain't gonna faint or nothing?"

Sonny nodded. Even though he held tightly to Bobby's arm, he walked with a determination that was absent before. Once again, when they reached the noisy street, the women sitting there moved to let them pass. Bobby heard them whisper as he and Sonny walked by. They headed for 8th Avenue.

On nice summer days, when Charlotte worked the day shift, she would walk the eight blocks in less than an hour. At other times she would walk the two long cross-town blocks, and then catch the Lenox Avenue bus the remaining six. Since neither Bobby nor Sonny had enough money for bus fare, they had to walk all the way. Sonny made it to the end of the first block without hesitation holding firmly onto Bobby's arm. When they came to 7th Avenue, however, the traffic noises seemed to paralyze him.

"You still want to go on?" Bobby asked as they stood at the curb.

As before, Sonny nodded. With each block, Bobby sensed the agony that both pushed Sonny on as well as made him want to turn back. But he didn't.

Finally, they arrived at the hospital entrance. It had taken them over two hours.

"We gotta think about how we gonna get in there," Bobby said looking up at the huge old red brick building. "Stay here while I go in and find out what room your mother's in."

Bobby left Sonny at the gate while he went up to the information desk. The receptionist, a young birdlike woman with glasses perched on the end of her nose, peered impatiently down at Bobby.

"Where's your parents? You're too young to be here alone."

He asked for Charlotte Henderson's room number.

"Excuse me, could you tell me if Dr. Bryan is in yet?" A man dressed in a dark suit and carrying a briefcase interrupted. He eased in front of Bobby and seemed to be in a hurry. Out of one pocket Bobby could see part of the doctor's stethoscope.

"Good morning, Dr. Lange," The receptionist smiled and efficiently responded to the doctor's inquiry. Before Bobby could make his request again, the telephone on the desk rang. Again the receptionist turned her attention away. Flipping through a stack of papers, she scanned a list before pressing a button on the phone base and switched the call.

Finally, after responding to several others who requested room numbers and directions, she turned back to Bobby. From her perch, she stared down at Bobby for a moment before giving him Charlotte's room number. Then, despite the suspicious look on her face, she cautioned him, "Remember, you're not allowed above the first floor." Bobby thanked her and headed for the exit, feeling her eyes following him as he went.

The boys walked around the building searching for a way to get in that wasn't locked or guarded. Just as they were about to give up, a side door opened and a group of nurses emerged. So absorbed in conversation, they failed to notice the boys slip in behind them. Luck was with them. The security guard had his back to the door as the boys managed to reach the stairs unseen. They walked up to the fifth floor and down the long corridor to Ward B. The floor nurses were also too busy to notice two boys, one sighted and the other blind, trying to look older than they really were. Down the rows of beds they walked until Bobby saw Charlotte. One heavily bandaged leg was suspended from a trapeze, the other beneath a white sheet, Charlotte seemed to be asleep as they approached the bed.

Bobby placed Sonny's hand on the bed railing and stood back as Sonny made his way to his mother's side.

Waking up with a start, "My baby!" she shouted when she saw him. She gathered him into her arms, tears streaming down her face.

"How did you get here?"

Then she saw Bobby. Bobby felt his stomach turn over. Had he done the right thing? he wondered. But when Charlotte reached out her other arm to him, he went to her. The smile on Sonny's face and Charlotte's strong arm around him, gave him the answer.

Mrs. Griffin is Missing

Chapter One

"Once I met Langston Hughes at a literary party. He had just published his poem 'The Weary Blues' and everybody flocked around him. It was so exciting." Her high-pitched voice sparkled with excitement. "In those days you never knew who you might meet at some of the events my husband, the late Mr. Griffin, took me to. When I met Langston Hughes, the most well-known poet of the Harlem Renaissance, well, all I can say is, it was an experience!" Mrs. Griffin smiled as if her memories were too private to share. Her eyes, focused on the distant past, were warm and glowing. "I bet you didn't know that Harlem was known throughout the world."

Bobby glanced at the clock. It was close to 8 p.m. and he knew his mother would soon be calling him, yet he didn't want to stop Mrs. Griffin; her stories held him transfixed for hours as if he were watching an exciting movie, one he didn't always understand. He scratched his head, crossed one leg over the other and retied the lace on his dirty sneaker. His hair was thick and matted and unless his mother made him, he seldom combed it. Like his father, he had a dark complexion and dimples. He got his abundant energy from his mother. An imaginative eleven year old, he saw adventure in everything. Shifting his position on her comfortable sofa, he glanced over at his friend Sonny who, like himself, sat spellbound. Sonny, too, was eleven. Visually handicapped since he was very young, Sonny was slightly taller than Bobby and much thinner. Because of his mother Charlotte who tried to shelter him from the outside world by creating a sanctuary inside their apartment, he was well read beyond his age. His almond colored skin was smooth except for the dark circles beneath his eyes. His hair was fine textured and always neatly brushed unlike Bobby's. As their friendship developed, so too, did Sonny's spirit for adventure.

"Oh my, it's getting late," Mrs. Griffin said. "I'd better let you children go. I get so carried away." She pushed the loose gray strands of hair back into the bun perched neatly on top of her head. She was the neighborhood mentor, a wise counselor who took it upon herself not only to teach the children about their heritage, and help them with their schoolwork, but also, nurture whatever talent she observed in them and tried to improve their social skills. To the adults, she was the one they called on for advice if they had problems with their children or other family matters. They knew she was there to help.

In her seventies, Mrs. Griffin, stood just under 5 ft. and weighed about 100 pounds. Except for reading glasses, her eyesight was excellent, and though she was in good health, lately she'd had a touch of arthritis in her hands. Always with a smile on her face, she made everyone who came to her feel special.

Bobby carried the empty glasses to the kitchen and rinsed them out. When he returned, Mrs. Griffin offered him and Sonny the remaining cookies.

"Take some for your folks. Tomorrow I'll bake you both an apple pie. And I'll tell you about Marcus Garvey and the Universal Negro Improvement Association."

"Who was he?" asked Sonny.

"He started the Back-to-Africa Movement. He even purchased a ship to transport American Negroes to the continent to form our own community. But I'll tell you more about him tomorrow."

"Wasn't that the time they use to have those big parades down Lenox Avenue?" Bobby asked. "I saw pictures in an old newspaper about them," thankful that his father saved old newspapers, magazines, and other objects others would have thrown away.

"That's right, Bobby. Your interest in history is commendable. I just wish all young people were as interested. How are you doing with your schoolwork? Are you remembering to enunciate your words clearly?"

"Yes Ma'am," Bobby muttered. "My teachers say I'm doing much better."

She turned to Sonny. "Don't forget to come by for your piano lessons at three. Have you remembered to practice?"

"Yes, Mrs. Griffin. I know the piece by heart." He held Bobby's arm as they walked to the door.

"I know you do. You have a natural gift for music. One day you'll make us all very proud." She patted both boys on their heads.

Mrs. Griffin pulled her shawl up around her shoulders. "Winter is in the air," she said.

"We'll have to get Mr. Brown to send up more heat."

At the door King Tut, her Abyssinian cat, suddenly appeared.

"There you are! Where have you been all day?" Mrs. Griffin reached down for him, but he slipped pass her. Releasing Sonny's hand from his arm, Bobby caught the fleeing cat just before it dashed under the sofa. He picked him up and brought him back to Mrs. Griffin who stroked his thick golden fur. As Bobby led Sonny up to his apartment, they heard Mrs. Griffin gently scolding King Tut.

The hallway smelled of a mixture of fried fish, baking bread, and rotting garbage, pickup was days away. The lights were so dim, Bobby could hardly see in front of him. He could have walked the halls blindfolded, though, having lived in this building all his life. Deep shadows enveloped the apartment doors they passed.

"You want to come in and listen to a few records?" Sonny asked when they reached his door.

"Not tonight. I'm kinda tired," Bobby said. "Your mother be working late tonight?"

"Just until nine. But I don't mind being alone. I'm use to it."

Taking the key from around his neck, Sonny let himself into the darkened apartment.

"See you tomorrow."

"See you," Bobby said as he started up to his own apartment. The third floor lights were out as usual. To still the uneasiness he always felt when alone among the shadows, Bobby pretended to be in one of the many parades led by Marcus Garvey down Lenox Avenue. Playing an imaginary trombone, he marched up the steps humming loudly and moving his arms back and forth. When he reached his door, he rapped on it in staccato.

"Who is it?" Brenda yelled.

"It's me."

"Who's me?" At thirteen, Brenda seemed to take great pleasure in tormenting her brother.

"Open up! and stop playing!"

Reluctantly, the door opened and was quickly slammed shut. Within minutes, the hallway was quiet except for a cacophony of sounds that floated from behind each apartment door. In Apartment 2C Sonny listened to his jazz records as he prepared for bed. His collection of blues, rock and roll, classical and jazz records would make the most avid collector envious. His mother Charlotte in an attempt to protect her son from the world, had supplied him with enough books and music to satisfy the most inquisitive. Last Christmas she had surprised him with an upright piano she'd purchased from a second-hand store. Mrs. Griffin had nurtured his musical abilities, and Bobby had helped him overcome his fear of going outside.

Upstairs, Bobby and Brenda carried on their usual argument about whose turn it was to dry the dishes until Mr. Thompson hushed them. After putting away her photograph albums, Mrs. Griffin sat down and played "Peace in the Valley" on her upright, her voice blending harmoniously with her playing. In answer to someone banging on the radiator, Mr. Brown shoveled a bit more coal into the furnace. Hours later, long after everyone was asleep, Sonny was awakened momentarily by a loud cry from King Tut followed by a door slamming. He got up and went to the bathroom, stopping by his mother's room to listen for her. Comforted by her gentle snoring, he returned to his room and quickly fell back to sleep. It was 3 a.m.

Chapter Two

*B*right and early, Bobby, dressed in faded blue jeans and his father's old sweatshirt, was down at Sonny's apartment. He loved weekends when there was no school and he could sleep late. However, this morning Mrs. Thompson needed a few breakfast items from the corner store, so before 9 a.m. Bobby, armed with his grocery list, knocked at Sonny's door.

"Since you're going, let me send Sonny along to pick up some things for me, if you don't mind," Charlotte said. Securing her duster firmly around her bulky frame, she swished to the kitchen and scribbled out her list. After reading it to Sonny, she handed it to him along with some change.

"Wear your hat," she told Sonny as the boys were leaving. "Don't want you catching a cold." Sonny protested but to no avail. Refusing Bobby's arm, he started out.

"I'm learning my way. I can make it to the front door by myself now."

"That's great!" Bobby responded walking in front of him as Sonny felt along the wall for the banister. "I'll tell you if somebody left any cans or bottles on the stairs, though it's so dark, I probably wouldn't see 'em myself."

"You think we should stop by Mrs. Griffin's to see if she needs anything?" Sonny asked as they passed her door.

"Good idea." Bobby knocked on Mrs. Griffin's door. The sound reverberated throughout the hallway. After several minutes with no answer they went on.

"She must be out or something."

"Or in the bathroom. That's okay. We'll stop by later."

Della's Corner Store had few shoppers as the day was young, and besides, most people who wanted more than the limited selections the store carried and at much lower prices went to the Super Market on 8th Avenue. After getting the items his mother requested, Bobby helped Sonny with his. On the way home with the groceries in tow, the boys stopped by the Odeon Theater to see what was playing. The main feature was "King Solomon's Mine." The second picture was one neither had heard of. It was in black and white. To round off the day's attractions were the usual assortment of cartoons. Colorful posters were tacked up all over the lobby, advertising attractions coming soon—in all their "splendor and breathtaking excitement." After agreeing to come back later, the boys walked on.

They strolled leisurely through the park stopping a few minutes to listen to the bongo players having their Saturday jam session. It was a staying-outside day, the air crisp enough to need a jacket, yet still warm with memories of Indian summer. Suddenly remembering the purpose of this excursion, they started home. As they passed Mrs. Griffin's door, once again Bobby gave it a loud rap. Still no answer.

"You sure took your time," Mrs. Thompson scolded Bobby as she removed the lukewarm milk and softened butter from the bag. Mrs. Thompson, who worked as a beautician, standing on her feet for long hours, was a hard working woman in her early 30's. Petite with brown eyes, a lovely heart-shaped face, her complexion was the color of walnut. Her short hair was uneven and limp as a result of too much pressing. By nature, she was optimistic and energetic. She could be stern at times though always ready to listen to her two children Bobby and Brenda.

"I stopped by Mrs. Griffin's house to see if she wanted anything from the store but she didn't answer the door," Bobby said.

"She was probably asleep or gone out."

"But she don't hardly ever go out."

"Maybe she didn't hear you," Mrs. Thompson responded patiently as she put away the groceries, took out a carton of eggs and began to prepare breakfast.

"I guess not." Bobby watched her a moment, then he asked, "Mama, can I have some money for the movies?"

"Did you make up your bed and straighten your room?"

Bobby nodded though his idea of a clean room was not the same as his mother's.

Mrs. Thompson reached into her apron pocket and handed him some change.

"Set the table, wake your dad and call Brenda."

After breakfast, Bobby hurried down to Sonny's and together they made their way over to the Odeon theater, a few blocks away. Saturday was movie day. At noon the theater opened to hundreds of enthusiastic youngsters all eager to spend six hours watching two feature films, twelve cartoons, coming attractions, newsreels and Flash Gordon action serial. Bobby and Sonny were among them.

By the time they got out, it was dark and several degrees colder. Sonny wished he'd worn his scarf and gloves like his mother told him. Charlotte was always trying to baby him, he'd complained. Bobby, on the other hand, was warm from the excitement of the movies. It was all Sonny could do to hold onto Bobby's gesturing arm as his friend relived the most action-filled scenes.

The next day they didn't hear Mrs. Griffin singing spirituals as she did every Sunday, nor did they see her on her way to church.

That evening Bobby waited for Sonny to finish dinner before he went downstairs. When Sonny told him that Mrs. Griffin hadn't answered the door for his piano lessons that afternoon, Bobby began to feel uneasy. If there was one thing you could say about Mrs. Griffin, it was that she never forgot appointments.

"You must be punctual and always strive to meet your obligations," he recited what she had told him many times.

Holding herself up as a role model, she took it upon herself to mold the neighborhood children's character. She taught them diction as well as piano and voice lessons. Also she attempted to teach them how to carry themselves like young ladies and gentlemen.

"Do you think she'd go anywhere without letting us know?"

"I wouldn't think so. Maybe she went to visit relatives"

"Uh, uh. As far as I know, she don't have no relatives. She been living here since before I was born and she never mentioned no relatives."

"Well, there's nothing we can do tonight," Sonny said.

"I sure miss hearing about Marcus Garvey and eating her apple pie."

"I missed my piano lessons."

"Maybe she went to visit some friends for the weekend," they concluded.

*   *   *   *

Coming from school the following day, Bobby rapped at Mrs. Griffin's door as he passed. He would have been surprised if she had answered. That evening as he took the garbage out, he saw King Tut sitting outside her door, meowing and scratching at the metal frame.

"Here kitty, kitty," he called, however, King Tut dashed away before Bobby could catch him.

After doing his homework Bobby went down to Sonny's house.

"Something's wrong." He told Sonny about seeing Mrs. Griffin's cat scratching at the door.

"She wouldn't go nowhere without taking King Tut with her," he said as more proof that something was out of the ordinary.

"Today as I was coming in from school, a man was standing at her door," Sonny said. "I could smell Old Spice shaving lotion. Mama's old boyfriend use to wear it."

"Did he say anything?"

"No, he coughed, though."

"Listen, do you think your mom would mind if you kept King Tut here until Mrs. Griffin come back? So he won't be sleeping in the street, starving or maybe even getting hit by a car. I'd take him but Brenda's scared of cats and my dad starts sneezing soon as he gets near fur."

"I could ask," Sonny said, thinking how nice it would be to have a pet even if it would only be for a little while. "I don't think my mother would mind."

"Tomorrow, soon as I get home, let's go peek through her window. For all we know, she coulda had a accident or something."

Sonny hesitated. "I don't know about that. Maybe we should ask Mr. Brown if he knows anything."

"Tell you what. First I'll peek through the window. If I don't see nothing, then we'll ask Mr. Brown."

Bobby felt excited as he usually did when his curiosity was aroused.

"We should start a detective agency. We could be like the Hardy Boys. Picture this 'Bobby and Sonny Detective Agency. No case is too big or too small for us.' Like it?"

Sonny laughed. "What can a blind guy like me do?"

"You got the brains and I got the….Come to think of it, what do I got?"

"You got the nose—nosy. Get it?"

They both laughed.

*   *   *   *

Bobby could hardly wait for school to end. It seemed as if each minute passed as slowly as an hour, and more than once his teacher admonished him for not paying attention. As soon as the three o'clock bell rang, he dashed from the building, ignoring his school buddies who yelled for him to join them in a basketball game on the yard. Running the five blocks from P.S. 80 down 139th St., across Seventh Avenue to his block, he dashed up the steps barely waiting for the neighborhood gossips to move from the entranceway.

"Well, where are you going in such a rush, *Mr.* Thompson?" Mrs. Mobley called after him. "Almost knocked me over!"

"Excuse me, Ma'am. I was just hurrying home to do my homework."

"Sonny's not home yet. Or at least I haven't seen his bus," she continued as Bobby rushed from hearing distance.

"Kids nowadays always rushing about like chickens with their heads cut off," Mrs. Vincent observed. The others nodded in agreement.

Bobby stopped in front of Sonny's door and knocked their secret signal. He didn't think to ask the women on the stoop about Mrs. Griffin. They seemed to know everything that went on in the block. Like his mother, Bobby knew Mrs. Griffin didn't care much about those busybodies. To tell them of his fears would be giving them more to gossip about. Only as a last resort would he ask them if they heard anything, he decided. No one answered Sonny's door so Bobby went upstairs to wait.

After a half hour, he couldn't stand waiting any longer. Glad that nosy Brenda wasn't home yet, he opened the back window and looked. Down in the yard, he saw Mr. Brown, the super, hauling discarded furniture from one side of the yard to the other. Bobby could have gone down the stairs and around to the back, but then he'd surely run into Mr. Brown and he wasn't a man to be fooled with. A slow moving man of 60 with a gruff voice, he acted as if he hated kids, always yelling and telling parents whenever one of them did something he or she shouldn't.

Bobby waited until Mr. Brown was out of sight and stepped out onto the fire escape. Because Mrs. Griffin's window was on the ground floor, Bobby had to jump from where the ladder stopped, about three feet from the ground, and he had to do it without Mr. Brown noticing him. The smell of garbage was particularly strong down there. Bobby held his nose as he crept up to Mrs. Griffin's window. As he reached over to peer into the glass, he stopped in his tracks.

The window was open!

Chapter Three

"*B*ut Mrs. Griffin would never leave her window open, especially living on the first floor," Sonny said later that afternoon.

"But it was. Not all the way, but enough for somebody to get inside." Bobby was out of breath as he told Sonny what he saw.

"Did you go in?" Sonny asked.

Bobby nodded. "I was scared, but I climbed in. All I could think of was she could be in there sick or something."

"Well?" Sonny waited impatiently for Bobby to go on. "Did you find anything?"

"No, nothing much. The place was neat like she always keep it. Except there was some dishes in the sink."

"Anything else?"

Bobby shrugged. "I didn't notice nothing." He hadn't stayed more than five minutes because somebody was knocking on the door.

"We gotta go back down there," Sonny said. "Did you close the window when you left?"

"I closed it and pulled down the shade, but it ain't locked."

"We'll go later tonight. My mom works late. Can you get away?"

"I'll try."

That evening, Bobby told his parents he and Sonny were working on a project together. Mr. Thompson nodded and continued to read his paper. Mrs. Thompson told him not to be late. Brenda, however, questioned him. What was the project? What was it for? How long would it take to finish? Finally he told her to mind her own business and ran out the door. Sisters were such a pain.

While Sonny went down the stairs, Bobby crept down the fire escape again. The light from the moon and those from the windows of all the buildings that bordered the yard made it easier for Bobby to see his way. Mr. Brown was nowhere in sight. Climbing into Mrs. Griffin's apartment, Bobby closed the curtains, flipped the light switch, and rushed to the door to let Sonny in.

"Where you want me to start?" Bobby asked as they stood in Mrs. Griffin's living room.

"Start from one side of the room and tell me everything you see."

Mrs. Griffin's living room was furnished modestly. Her furniture was old but of good quality. Crocheted doilies covered the arms of the chairs and tabletop. Fading photographs of her family and friends stood on the mantelpiece. On top of her upright piano were books of poetry, novels, biographies, folktales and books on etiquette. In one corner stood her china cabinet filled with her fine china, gold leaf plates, cups trimmed in gold, and a silver tea set.

Hesitatingly, the boys ventured into her bedroom. Her bed covers were folded down neatly, yet it didn't look as if anyone had slept in the bed. Her closet was stuffed with clothes. Suitcases and boxes crowned the top. Though neat and orderly, it seemed as if every available space was crammed full. Mrs. Griffin's long life stretched the tiny apartment to its limits. If anything were missing, Bobby couldn't tell. The dress Mrs. Griffin wore the last time they'd seen her was hung just inside the door. Her shoes sat beneath them. On the dresser, her pocketbook rested half hidden beneath a scarf.

"I don't see her pajamas," Bobby said.

"Women like Mrs. Griffin don't wear pajamas. They wear night-gowns, I think."

"Well, I don't see no nightgown or bedroom slippers. My mother always keeps her nightclothes spread out on her bed. She says it's easier to find."

"Anything else?" Sonny asked.

Nothing seemed out of the ordinary except no nightgown or bed-room slippers.

"Let's check the bathroom."

All the necessary items were there as far as Bobby could tell.

"What about her toothbrush? If she was going away, even overnight, she'd take her toothbrush."

"Nope, her toothbrush is in the holder, unless she got a extra one. Or unless she don't need one, you know, maybe she got false teeth."

"Doesn't matter. She'd still need a toothbrush. She must've left in a hurry."

Their inspection yielded little results. The boys returned to where they started.

"Look here," Bobby said, picking up a folded piece of paper from beneath the coffee table. "Coming Soon to Tiny's Haven, the Dwight Hopkins Trio," he read.

"What would Mrs. Griffin be doing with an ad from a nightclub?" Sonny asked. Suddenly he sniffed the air. "Smells like somebody's been smoking. Do you smell it?"

Bobby searched around until he saw it. On the coffee table, a cigarette butt crushed out in one of Mrs. Griffin's good plates.

"Do you think maybe it was one of her friends?" Sonny asked.

"I don't think so. Mrs. Griffin don't allow nobody to smoke around her. That's what my daddy told me."

"We'd better go," Sonny said nervously.

"Yeah, I think so, too." Bobby also felt uneasy.

Chapter Four

"*D*id your mother check the register at Harlem Hospital to see if Mrs. Griffin was there?" Mrs. Thompson asked Sonny as she set a stack of pancakes before him.

Because Charlotte had worked late the night before, instead of waiting for her to wake, Sonny had gone upstairs to Bobby's.

"She checked but didn't come up with anything. She said she'd call around to other hospitals today if she got a chance."

"I don't know why you children are causing all this fuss. Mrs. Griffin probably went out of town to see some relative," Mr. Thompson said. He scooped the remains of his sunny-side-up eggs into his mouth and washed them down with coffee.

"But she don't have no relatives as far as I know," Bobby responded.

"**Any** relatives," Mrs. Thompson corrected.

"As far as I know," Brenda mimicked. "You think you know everything. Then, how was she born without no relatives?" She laughed. "Gotcha!"

"I'm starting to worry too, Joe," Mrs. Thompson said. "Ida Mae's folks died almost ten years before she moved here. She had a brother, but if I remember correctly, he was killed in the war."

"That don't mean anything's happened to her. She could have gone to visit friends. I think you all are worryin' over nothing." He got up from the table. "Gotta run down to a meeting at the Lodge. Be back as soon as I can." He kissed his wife on her cheek, pulled one of Brenda's braids, and ruffled Bobby's hair. "Boy, you need a hair cut. Remind me when I come back to take you to the barbershop."

As he passed Sonny's chair, he patted him lightly on the back. A few moments later, they heard the door shut and the lock being thrown into place.

"Well, Mama, what do you think me and Sonny should do if she ain't in the hospital?" Bobby asked.

Mrs. Thompson resisted the temptation to correct his grammar. "I'm not sure. Maybe she has gone to visit friends like your father said. Why don't we wait a bit. She'll turn up. Who would want to harm that sweet old lady?" She removed the plates from the table. "Brenda, it's your turn to do the dishes."

"Let's go see Mr. Brown," Sonny suggested.

"I guess we better." Bobby was reluctant to tackle the man who had been responsible for his many punishments. Mr. Brown seemed to have eyes in the back of his head.

They found the super in the basement pulling the coal chute into position for delivery of a new supply. Just as Bobby and Sonny walked in, Mr. Brown hollered up to the truck to send down its cargo. The din of coal sliding down the chute filled the basement with so much noise it was impossible to carry on a conversation. Standing at a safe distance, the boys waited patiently. When the noise ceased and the dust settled, they approached the old man. His back was to them. He started when Bobby called his name.

"What'chu two doin' down here?" he said, his gruff voice scraping fear along their spines. "Don't you know you ain't suppose to trespass!"

Gathering his courage, Sonny told him of their mission.

"Do I look like a information service? Why you want to know anyway? What you boys got up your sleeves?"

He peered down at them through red-rimmed eyes.

"We haven't seen her in d'days and we was w'wondering if she moved out?" he stammered.

"Why would she move out. Her rent's paid up to next month. Get up out of here! I got better things to do then fool with you kids. You should mind your own business, that's what, 'stead of tending to other peoples...." His voice trailed off as he swept up the coal chunks that had missed the bin.

Bobby and Sonny emerged into the sunlight discouraged but grateful for clean air.

"Well, what do we do now?" Bobby asked as they sat down on the chairs on the stoop.

"We know wherever she went she didn't go on her own because she wouldn't have left King Tut alone. And she wouldn't have left her window open."

"We know she ain't in Harlem Hospital."

"And since she's paid her rent, she's planning to come back."

"And what do you two boys think you're doing sitting in our chairs?"

Mrs. Vincent loomed over them, her hands on her hips. Bobby raised his eyes slowly over her floppy house slippers, her skinny ankles and muscular calves, her angular frame, the pins fastened to her thick sweater, and looked into her frowning brown eyes. He jumped up, pulling Sonny with him.

"We're sorry," he apologized. What could they have been thinking to sit on the women's chairs? Mrs. Vincent took her place, followed by Mrs. Mobley who cast a dark eye at them. Sonny and Bobby found seats on the overturned garbage cans that, having been emptied of their contents, lined the curb waiting for Mr. Brown's removal.

Overnight the temperature had dropped. Yet nothing short of snow would keep the women from their usual post. Likewise, a group of young girls were playing hopscotch a couple of doors down from the building. The few pedestrians hurried along the sidewalk, their collars turned up against the chilly wind.

"Like I was telling you last night. The man was as handsome as could be. I still can't see why he was foolin' around with that homely woman," said Mrs. Mobley.

"I don't believe they was married," Mrs. Vincent responded. "All I can say is I'd never marry a musician. No good. That's all they is. Their true love is their music.

"Girl," Mrs. Mobley eyed her, "how you know so much about musicians? I thought your husband was a mechanic."

"I wasn't always married to Henry," Mrs. Vincent snickered.

Bobby and Sonny sat in silence, each thinking over the events of the past several days.

"Anyway, they only stayed here about a month. Next thing I knew, they was gone. Disappeared just like that."

Mrs. Mobley's last sentence caught Bobby's attention.

"Disappeared…just like Mrs. Griffin," he thought.

"Mrs. Griffin disappeared, too," he said without thinking, interrupting the women's conversation.

"What'chu talking about, boy?" Mrs. Vincent scolded. "Didn't your mama tell you not to eavesdrop on other folks' conversation?"

"He didn't mean to listen." This time Sonny apologized. "We were wondering if you'd seen Mrs. Griffin. We haven't seen her around lately."

"How should we know?" Mrs. Mobley replied. "Don't you boys have anything to do? Why don't you go down the street and play."

Taking the hint, Bobby and Sonny moved away from the building to the corner store and sat down on the curb in front.

"I think we'd better go back to Mrs. Griffin's apartment one more time," said Sonny. "There's got to be something we missed."

"You're right, but first we gotta wait until the coast is clear."

Chapter Five

*I*t wasn't as easy getting into Mrs. Griffin's apartment as it was before. The window, though not locked, had slammed shut. Bobby managed to pry it open enough to get his hands inside. The boys climbed in and Bobby quickly closed the curtains and turned on the lights. The room was as they had left it; the dishes lay unwashed in the sink. On the coffee table in the living room sat the plate with its half-smoked cigarette. Beside it lay the flyer advertising an event at Tiny's Haven.

"Read that to me again," Sonny asked.

"It says, 'Coming Soon, the smooth sounds of the Dwight Hopkins Trio.'" Bobby read the entire flyer including the price of admission.

"Wasn't Mrs. Mobley and Mrs. Vincent talking about a musician living here?"

"I wasn't paying no attention, but I think they said something like that."

"D'you think there's a connection?"

"I don't know, but maybe we better check it out."

The boys examined the room further and finding nothing else, they turned off the lights and started toward the front door. No sooner had Bobby reached for the knob when he heard a key being inserted into the lock. His heart skipped.

"Quick, we gotta hide!"

Bobby pushed Sonny into the hall closet. The door opened slowly and who should enter but Mr. Brown, the Super. Bobby cracked the closet door and watched Mr. Brown explore Mrs. Griffin's kitchen. Stopping at the cupboard, he removed a glass and reaching into another cupboard, pulled out the bottle of wine Mrs. Griffin kept for special occasions like when the neighbor's son graduated from medical school. Mrs. Griffin had thrown a party for him and had invited Bobby's family along with a few others in the building. Mr. Brown poured himself a glass and drank it. He poured himself another and did the same. Then he filled the bottle with water and tightly capped it.

Passing near the closet where Bobby and Sonny hid, Mr. Brown slowly swayed into the living room.

"Wait here," Bobby whispered to Sonny as he dropped to his knees and crept quietly after Mr. Brown. Once in the living room, the super went over to Mrs. Griffin's record collection and began leafing through it. After selecting a record and putting it on the phonograph, Brown made himself comfortable in Mrs. Griffin's favorite chair, an overstuffed armchair that had its own vivid story, but Bobby couldn't remember the details. Taking out a cigar, he lit it, propped his feet up on her coffee table, and before the record had ended, he fell asleep, his loud snores cutting into the smooth sounds of Bobby Blue Bland.

"Come on. The coast is clear." Bobby pulled Sonny along, past the snoring Brown and towards the front door.

"Did you get the flyer?" Sonny asked once safely outside.

Bobby searched through his pockets. Then he remembered. He'd left it on the kitchen table when he'd tried to open the window.

He turned to go back in. When he reached the living room, he glanced over at the still-sleeping super. On tiptoes, he moved cautiously to the kitchen and grabbed the flyer. Just as he was about to cross into the living room, the record needle, caught in a groove, began to repeat a phrase.

"…and she left…and she left…and she left…"

Bobby froze.

Mr. Brown woke with a start, groaned and stretched. Bobby wasted no time hustling back to the door and quickly closing it behind him.

"We better go home. I'll call you later," he said to Sonny who was waiting by the banister. Bobby was just about to follow when the door opened and Mr. Brown stepped out. He jumped when he saw the young boy. Scowling, he said, "Just checking to see if everything was all right.

What'chu doing hanging around this door?"

"I was just passing," Bobby answered.

"Well, move along then." Mr. Brown grumbled as he shuffled down the opposite way.

Later that evening Bobby called Sonny. It was decided that the next day they would go over to Tiny's Haven and do some investigating.

Chapter Six

*T*iny's Haven was located on 7th Avenue and 137th Street. Once an elegant restaurant and nightclub on the order of the Baby Grand and Small's Paradise, it was the place sophisticated, well-heeled Blacks frequented. In the 1930's, Fletcher Henderson and his group were regulars there. During the 1940's it boasted a lineup of musicians such as Charlie Parker and Lester Young, and singers such as Ella Fitzgerald and Billie Holiday or Lady Day.

Now it was simply a nightclub that featured local and out-of-town groups. Though evidence of its luxurious past could still be seen, Tiny's patronage today consisted of workers who popped in for a quick drink between shifts, old-time gamblers, retired musicians, and in the evening, older couples who stopped by before going downtown for a movie.

After school the next day, Bobby and Sonny stood just outside the entrance to the nightclub. As it was early afternoon, few people were around.

"Are you sure we should go in there? Suppose they have us arrested," Sonny asked. He was also thinking about his mother and what she'd do if she found out he'd gone into a place like Tiny's Haven.

However, nothing could dissuade Bobby. Once his curiosity was aroused, he wouldn't stop until he was satisfied.

"They can't do that. All we want is some information. You wait here. I'll go in and investigate," he said leaving Sonny sitting on the fire hydrant near the curb.

It took Bobby a while to adjust to the dim lighting. He could just make out the tables with chairs stacked on them. The soft sounds of jazz came from a jukebox in the far corner of the room, and though the place was empty, the smell of alcohol and stale cigarettes lingered in the air. As his eyes became use to his surroundings, Bobby saw that the walls were covered with black and white photographs of well-known stars of the 1930's and 1940's. He recognized some of the faces from a book he'd seen at Mrs. Griffins. An autographed photo of Duke Ellington hung near the bar next to one of Sarah Vaughn. There was even one of Dizzy Gillespie blowing his horn, his cheeks puffed out, distorting his features. Mrs. Griffin had said that was his trademark. Bobby stared at them with fascination, momentarily forgetting his purpose.

"Hey kid, what are you doing in here?" A voice startled him into the present. "You don't look twenty-one to me." Bobby saw a young woman standing at a table next to the entrance. She smiled at him and through the dim light, he saw a handsome woman with a broad mouth and large teeth.

She wore a white blouse, and black pants, over which was an apron, white socks and black, comfortable shoes. Her hair was hidden under a small scarf. In her hand she held a large towel which she used to wipe each table before moving on to the next.

She repeated her question. Bobby nervously took the flyer from his pocket and handed it to her.

"I was looking for a friend. Mrs. Griffin."

"Does she play with this group?" the woman asked. She tapped the flyer with one long painted fingernail.

"No, I mean…Me and my friend found this in her apartment and…," he stumbled, feeling his stomach flip flop as he wondered whether he was making any sense; especially seeing the puzzled look on her face.

Handing the flyer back to him, she said, "Look kid, I don't know what you're talking about. And you better get out of here before Big Joe sees you. If he loses his license, you gonna have h…'cuse me, heck to pay."

Bobby glanced quickly around. the place was empty except for the two of them, and an old man sitting at the bar watching a football game.

At that moment, Bobby saw a huge man emerge from the back room. He looked like one of those Sumo wrestlers Bobby had seen on TV.

"Sadie, what's that kid doing in here?" His voice boomed over the music, deep and frightening. Bobby looked at the door measuring how long it would take him to reach it.

"He's trying to get a job with the "Dwight Hopkins Trio," she laughed again. "What instrument do you play?"

Bobby felt annoyed with her jokes, but it stopped Big Joe from coming over. He went behind the bar and sat down. Soon he was absorbed in the game and seemed to have forgotten Bobby's presence.

"Just kidding. The Trio will be here tonight. But you'd better get your father to come see them. Ain't no way you gonna get back in here. Now go on home. You too young to be hanging out in a place like this."

*   *   *   *

Sonny was anxiously waiting when Bobby came out. Before saying anything, Bobby stood still a moment to let his eyes adjust to the bright sunlight. Then after telling Sonny all that happened in Tiny's, they sat down on the curb to figure out what to do next.

What was the connection between the Dwight Hopkins Trio and Mrs. Griffin? She would be the last person to go into a place like Tiny's, and to see a jazz group? It just didn't make sense.

"Like the woman said, how are you gonna get in there tonight to talk to Dwight Hopkins? Maybe you could ask your father," Sonny suggested.

"My dad!" Bobby shook his head. "My folks gonna wonder what I was doing in a nightclub in the first place and where I got the flyer from. If I told them I been in Mrs. Griffin's place, I'd be in big trouble. No, I can't ask them for no help."

"You're right. We can't ask our parents. We're not suppose to be snooping into other people's business, they'd say."

Bobby glanced at the door of Tiny's just as someone emerged. Recognizing the man as the one who had been sitting at the bar watching football, Bobby's eyes followed him. An elderly gentleman in his late 60's or early 70's, he was small in statue, dark complexion and he walked as if he carried a heavy burden on his back. His glance met Bobby's and

· 44 ·

he smiled. Without thinking, Bobby smiled back. As he passed the boys, the man tipped his hat and went on his way. Bobby's eyes followed until the man was out of sight.

"Looks like we ran into another wall," Sonny was saying. "We better go home before it gets any later."

Chapter Seven

*I*t was growing dark by the time they reached home. Bobby looked up to see the lights on in his living room so he knew his parents were home. The "stoop" women were not in their usual spot, further indication that it was late. As they approached the stairs, they saw a man knocking at Mrs. Griffin's door. There was something familiar about him, the slump in his shoulders. Suddenly it hit him where he'd seen the man before.

"It's the man from Tiny's!" Bobby whispered pulling Sonny to the side.

Grateful now for the dark shadows, the boys huddled against the wall and waited.

"Shouldn't we do something?" Sonny whispered.

"Like what?"

"I don't know. Ask him something about Mrs. Griffin."

After knocking several times, the man turned to leave. Just as he neared the boys, he saw them. Startled, the man jumped back. Bobby stepped from the shadows. For an instant, the man's eyes grew wide with fear, then he smiled.

"Well, boys, we meet again. You're not following me, are you?" His voice was soft and husky and had a hint of a southern drawl. He continued to the outside door.

"We heard you knocking at Mrs. Griffin's door, and…" Sonny began.

"Do you mind if I sit down?" the man interrupted with a long sigh, as he sat down on one of the chairs on the stoop. "There," he sighed again. "I'm not as young as I use to be. By the way my name is Williams, Howard Williams. And you are?"

Bobby introduced himself and Sonny and, with growing anxiety, waited while Mr. Williams pulled a pipe from his pocket, slapped the bowl against his palm, filled it with tobacco and lit it. Small puffs of smoke filled the air before Mr. Williams spoke.

"Now, start from the beginning. What's this about Mrs. Griffin?"

"She's a friend of ours. We haven't seen her in a long time and we were worried," Sonny said.

Mr. Williams looked down at his pipe. Then he scratched his head. "I'm a friend of hers, too, and I was beginning to worry when I hadn't heard from her."

Sonny explained what had happened the night before Mrs. Griffin disappeared, how she'd promise to make them an apple pie and tell them about the Negro Improvement Association and Marcus Garvey.

"I know she didn't plan to go away. Unless it was something that happened all of a sudden."

"And she wouldn't be leaving King Tut out in the street," Bobby added.

"King Tut? Oh yes, her cat," Mr. Williams said with a smile. "Tell me. What were you doing at Tiny's Haven earlier today? Did it have anything to do with Mrs. Griffin?"

The boys were reluctant to tell him that they'd been in Mrs. Griffin's apartment, but how else could they explain the flyer and the cigarette they'd found. Finally Bobby told him how they'd gone into her apartment hoping to find some clue to her disappearance.

"Dwight Hopkins Trio. Hmmm. She never mentioned any one like that to me." Mr. Williams thought a while. "I just remembered. Did you talk to Mrs. Griffin's niece. She may know where Mrs. Griffin is?"

"Her niece?" Bobby asked. "We didn't know she got a niece. Where do she live? Do you know her address?" He asked, his hopes rising.

"Nope, I only met her once. I think she was living here at the time."

"Living here?" Sonny couldn't remember meeting anyone at Mrs. Griffin's and certainly not a niece.

"Bobby! Sonny!" Mrs. Thompson's voice punctuated the darkness. Bobby looked up to see his mother leaning out the third floor window.

"We down here," he shouted up at her.

"Do you know what time it is? You know better than to stay out this late. Dinner's on the table...." She went on even as she drew her head in.

"Mr. Williams, we gotta go," Sonny explained. "But could we get in touch with you to talk more about Mrs. Griffin?"

"Certainly, boys. And let me know whatever you find out." He searched his pockets. Taking out an envelope, he tore a piece from it and wrote down his phone number. He handed it to Bobby.

"Well, what do you think?" Bobby asked Sonny as they rushed into the building.

"At least it's good to know we're not alone."

*   *   *   *

The next day, as soon as school was over, Bobby and Sonny met at Sonny's apartment. They decided to call Mr. Williams to learn more information about Mrs. Griffin's niece. The only thing he could tell them was that on one of his visits, he had met a young woman there. Mrs. Griffin had introduced her as her niece from Virginia. She told him how happy she was. She didn't think she had any living relatives and to have one living so close was a welcomed surprise. He didn't think to ask her more about it.

"She's like the daughter I never had," Mrs. Griffin had said.

"How long ago did she live here?" Bobby asked. Mr. Williams didn't think it was that long ago. Maybe a few months ago. After that one time, Mrs. Griffin never mentioned her again. Mr. Williams could tell them nothing more, but he promised to get in touch with them again if he thought of anything else.

"If Mrs. Griffin's niece was living here a few months ago, somebody should know," Sonny said.

"Yeah, and I know who knows everything that go on in this building. The problem is who's gonna question them?"

"Not me," Sonny said quickly. "I'm scared of Mr. Brown."

"I was talking about Mrs. Mobley and Mrs. Vincent. I guess we better ask Mr. Brown, too. If you talk to him, I'll ask them."

Sonny reluctantly agreed.

The boys decided to meet later that evening to compare notes.

Chapter Eight

"Why you wanna know, Bobby Thompson? What's it got to do with you?" Mrs. Mobley answered when Bobby approached her that evening. She was sitting alone which made it a little easier for him.

"Yeah, I saw her," Mrs. Mobley said after Bobby explained his interest. "I didn't know she was Mrs. Griffin's niece though. They never said nothing to me; you know how some people are. And I didn't see where it was up to me to be butting into other people's business."

"But you saw them together?" Bobby asked.

Mrs. Mobley shifted in her chair and thought for a moment.

"I don't remember, but I'll ask Mrs. Vincent." Her eyes softened as she leaned towards Bobby. "You think somebody kidnapped Mrs. Griffin? And you think maybe that young girl had something to do with it?"

"Lucy, what you talking so secretly to this boy about?" Mrs. Vincent suddenly appeared in the doorway. Bobby jumped up from her seat and moved to the side.

"Do you remember that young girl who was married to that musician who lived here a few months ago?" Mrs. Mobley asked.

"I seem to recall. Yeah, so what?"

"Bobby here says she was Mrs. Griffin's niece."

"Was she? Uh huh. I believe she was or so she said," Mrs. Vincent said.

"You still running around trying to find that old woman? Didn't I tell you she probably went to visit some relatives in Virginia?"

"How did you know she was from Virginia?" Mrs. Mobley asked? "I never knew that."

"I remember seeing a letter addressed to her from Virginia."

"And how did you just happen to see Mrs. Griffin's mail?" Mrs. Mobley asked, her voice rising.

An argument was developing as Mrs. Mobley accused Mrs. Vincent of snooping. While they both loved to gossip, they did not like it if one of them knew more about a subject than the other.

Since the women seemed to have forgotten Bobby's presence, he kept quiet and listened. After a while, not learning anything new, he slipped away.

*   *   *   *

Meanwhile, Sonny was presented with a prime opportunity to question Mr. Brown. That afternoon, he came to Sonny's apartment to fix a clogged sink. As he worked, Sonny asked him about Mrs. Griffin's niece. At first Mr. Brown grumbled as he always did whenever he was asked to repair anything in a tenant's apartment. But as he worked, his tongue would loosen and he would ramble on and on about everything under the sun, not stopping until he had completed the job. The only problem was it was difficult to follow his train of thought. In answer to Sonny's question, Mr. Brown described each tenant's repair problems, the broken window in Apartment 5A, the plaster that had fallen in Apartment 3D, the cracked radiator in Apartment 4B.

"I don't know what they think I am, a workhorse. If it ain't one thing, it's another," he grumbled.

Knowing that if he waited long enough Mr. Brown was sure to answer his question, Sonny didn't press him. Instead he waited patiently, concentrating on Mr. Brown's maze-like conversation. When he'd almost finished, sure enough, Mr. Brown spoke of Florence Hopkins and her musician husband, Dwight.

"A mousy looking woman if ever I saw one. Wouldn't look at me straight, always shifting her eyes, looking down at the ground like she was still on the plantation. Now that husband of hers, man, could he play sax. Reminded me of Bird*. Had to go up there a couple of times because the neighbors complained. After that he came down to my place to practice. Sweet. That's what it was, sweet."

He turned the water on and watched it swirl down the now cleared drain. After rinsing off the plunger, and drying his hands on Charlotte's kitchen towel, Mr. Brown gathered up his tool case and started for the door.

"One night, a couple of months ago, they just up and left. Slipped out without paying the rent. Ain't seen them since. Saw that little mousy wife of his coming out of that Mrs. Griffin's apartment once. When she saw me, though, she took off in the opposite direction. Must'a thought I was gonna get after her about the money she owed. Ain't none of my business. I don't go chasing after nobody lessen they owe me money. I don't own this building; I just do what I'm paid to do, haul garbage, stoke the furnace, and fix things that break. They don't pay me enough to…." his voice trailed off as he moved down the stairs.

*   *   *   *

That evening, Bobby and Sonny got together to see what they'd come up with. Since Charlotte would not be home until 8 p.m., she had prepared a pot of stew and left it on the stove for Sonny's dinner. Together Bobby and Sonny finished off the stew.

"We know this woman Florence who claimed to be Mrs. Griffin's niece was married to Dwight Hopkins, the leader of a band that played at Tiny's Haven."

"And we know they came from Virginia and that Mrs. Griffin got a letter from somebody in Virginia," added Bobby enthusiastically.

"So where do we go from there?" Sonny asked, stroking King Tut's head. The cat purred comfortably in his arms. "Maybe we should ask Mr. Williams if he knows anything about Mrs. Griffin and Virginia."

---

* *Charlie Parker (1920–1955) nicknamed Yardbird or Bird, was one of the greatest jazz saxophonist ever.*

"Yeah, I guess we could," Bobby glanced at his Mickey Mouse watch. "It's getting late and I got a math test to study for. If I don't pass it, my dad is gonna be mad."

Since they had been working on the case, Bobby's grades had been slipping. He was too involved to concentrate on anything outside of finding Mrs. Griffin. Compared to that, everything else was boring. Nevertheless, if he didn't put more time into his studies, his father had told him, he'd be grounded for a month of Sundays and with Christmas a month away…. Reluctantly, he went up to his apartment.

*   *   *   *

"Bout time you came home. Act like you don't live here no more," Brenda said, slamming the door behind him and rolling her eyes.

"Bobby, a Mr. Williams called. Said he wanted to invite you and Sonny to lunch on Saturday. Who is this Mr. Williams?" His mother waited patiently for Bobby to answer. He grabbed his books and plopped down in front of the television set before explaining.

When he saw that his mother was genuinely interested, he told her of his and Sonny's progress in trying to discover the whereabouts of Mrs. Griffin. The more he talked, the more excited he became. He told her about what they'd learned from Mrs. Mobley, Mrs. Vincent, and Mr. Brown.

"I remember seeing Mr. and Mrs. Hopkins a few times, too," said Mrs. Thompson. "I always thought there was something strange about them." As she described her suspicions, Bobby noticed a mischievous gleam in her eyes. One day, she added, she was almost tempted to eavesdrop on their conversation when she saw them arguing in the hall. If she was younger, Bobby thought watching his mother, she'd make a good detective like himself and Sonny. That was one of the things Bobby loved about his mother. She never made him feel that his insatiable curiosity was stupid. She always supported him in most of his adventures.

"Mama, I'm hungry and dinner's getting cold," Brenda whined from the kitchen. Bobby wasn't very hungry, having eaten a good portion of

Sonny's meal. Still he sat at the table and as dishes were being passed, took only a small amount of food. Everyone sat down and, after saying grace, ate their meal together as was the custom in the Thompson household.

As Mr. Thompson ate, he read his newspaper, lowering it from time to time to tell his wife about an interesting article he'd just read. Mrs. Thompson continued her inquiry into Bobby and Sonny's discoveries while Brenda glanced through a movie magazine hidden beneath the table.

"It says here they uncovered another nursing home scandal," Mr. Thompson said. "This one in New Jersey."

"I heard about it on the news," Mrs. Thompson responded. "Said they found people locked up in their rooms, some of them half starved to death." She shook her head. "I don't know how people can treat other people like that."

"Why can't they just leave?" Brenda asked. "That's what I'd do."

"People can't just sign themselves in and out of a nursing home whenever they choose," Mr. Thompson explained. "Usually people are placed there when they have no place else to turn, and they can't take care of themselves."

"In the old days, before nursing homes, folks would take care of their elderly relatives themselves, black folks particularly. You didn't just send your mother or father off to have others take care of them," Mrs. Thompson added. "Nowadays everything in our society is geared for the young. When you get old, society don't have any more use for you."

Bobby remembered that for years, up until she died, his grandmother had lived with them. She'd taught him so much in her quiet, unassuming way. He couldn't imagine his grandma in any place other than with the family.

"Did you check the nursing homes?" Mrs. Thompson asked.

"Check for what?" It took Bobby a few moments to bring his thoughts back to the present. His grandmother's death had left a void in his young life even though it had been several years ago.

"For Mrs. Griffin, knucklehead," Brenda shouted. Turning to her mother she asked, "Why would she be in a nursing home? Who would put her there?"

"It was just a thought. I can't imagine Ida Mae being in a nursing home without us knowing about it. Besides, Bobby and Sonny were at her house a short while ago."

"Well, it's worth checking into. If she is, we'd better do whatever we can to get her out," said Mr. Thompson.

Realizing that not only did he have his mother's support, but also his father's and even Brenda's, Bobby felt confident that they'd find Mrs. Griffin, somehow.

"That'll be our next step," he said firmly as he reached across the table for another piece of fried chicken.

Chapter Nine

Mr. Williams lived in a rooming house on Fifth Avenue and 126th Street. Once an attractive brownstone, inhabited by the well-to-do at the turn of the century, it had since been converted into a rooming house to accommodate as many residents as possible. Each rented a small room which served as living room, bedroom, and kitchen. One communal bathroom on each floor served the needs of the tenants on that floor. Evidence of fine workmanship could still be seen by anyone interested in architecture, the stain glass window, now cracked and dirty; the rich mahogany paneling and high ceilings, the gracefully curving banister. For the most part, however, the roomers, with more important things on their minds, could have cared less as long as the toilet worked and the water for baths was hot.

Bobby and Sonny walked slowly up the stairs to Mr. Williams's room on the third floor and knocked on the door. Mr. Williams greeted them with the same warm smile he had when they first met him.

Neat but cluttered, the room looked smaller than it was because of the amount of stuff Mr. Williams had accumulated over the years. A trunk and several suitcases were intermingled with boxes stacked in the corner. A clothes rack laden with pants, shirts and suit jackets stood in another corner. The full-size bed, however, took up much of the floor space. Though he shared the kitchen facilities and the bathroom with three other tenants on that floor, he kept a hot plate in his room to cook his meals.

"I hope you like Chinese food," he said as he opened the steaming cartons and placed them on the card table set up for lunch.

"You got your choice of pork fried rice, chop suey, and egg rolls. I get them from the restaurant on the corner and I thought you boys would like some."

As he talked, he dished out a large serving from each carton onto their plates and then filled his. While they ate, Mr. Williams talked about the days when he was a sleeping car porter traveling throughout the country.

"That's one way to see America cheap. Another way is to get a job on a ship. That's how Langston Hughes got to see the world. He worked as a cook on a ship. Yes indeed, that's one thing I'd like to do, see the world. Travel to all them foreign places." He shook his head regretfully and wiped his mouth. "But I'm getting too old for that. Time I settled down. That's why I went to see Ida Mae, uh, Mrs. Griffin. Wanted to ask her to marry me." He winked at Bobby.

"You must'a known Mrs. Griffin a long time," Sonny asked.

"Knew her before she met her husband. Met her in Virginia when she was a young thing. I was stopped over in Richmond for a week waiting for a new route when we met. Fell in love with her at first sight. Would've got married right then and there 'cept I had to move on. Not ready to settle down."

Bobby's eyes wandered the room. He cocked his head to read the names on the colored stickers on the trunk, some torn but still legible— New Mexico, Texas, Louisiana, California, and Chicago. He looked at the photos on the wall, black and white photos of a younger man in a World War I army uniform. One fading photograph of a large family standing in the yard in front of a ramshackle house.

"Next thing I knew, she'd married and moved North like so many colored folks did," Mr. Williams continued. "But we been in touch over the years. I'd send her a post card wherever I'd happen to be."

The afternoon sped by as the boys listened to Mr. Williams and asked him questions about his adventures. Sonny was particularly interested in what the places looked like. He'd read about California, but hearing about it from somebody who had actually been there was something else. "One of these days I'd like to take a trip out there. It must be great to live some place where it never snows or gets real cold."

Bobby was more interested in the people Mr. Williams met. "Did you meet Buck Rogers when you was in Hollywood?"

In his travels Mr. Williams had met many people, politicians, entertainers, musicians, and other professionals. His reminiscences reminded both boys of how much they missed Mrs. Griffin.

"Of all the places you've been, how come you chose Harlem to live?" Sonny asked.

"For one reason, this is where Ida Mae lives. And another reason, Harlem was thought to be the promise land. It's the place most unlike the South where you could get a good paying job, a nice place to stay, and live a fairly decent life. Lots of Negroes did the same thing, sold their land and came up to this here promise land hoping for a better life."

In his mind Bobby saw images of thousands of black people leaving the South and heading to the North with only the clothes on their backs, or carrying cardboard suitcases and in some cases, simply a paper bag filled with what little belongings they had; a long line, stretched across the horizon, trekking hundreds of miles to this small island called Harlem.

Because he'd lived all his life in Harlem, Bobby couldn't understand the fascination. Though he'd heard about its rich history, he didn't see it as any place special. Now what he'd really love to see was Hollywood, movie stars, the beach....

"Did Mrs. Griffin have land?" Sonny asked bringing Bobby back to the present.

"As a matter of fact, her parents left her well over 100 acres," said Mr. Williams. "I don't know what became of it when she moved North. Maybe it's still down there, I reckon. Sure would be a good place to retire to 'stead of living up here in these cramped rooms."

Soon it was time to leave. The afternoon shadows had lengthened and crept up the walls of the room. Mr. Williams's stories had held them captive all day, but in the end, they still had no clue as to Mrs. Griffin's whereabouts nor where her "supposed" niece might be. Despite the enjoyable company, Bobby and Sonny left Mr. Williams's feeling a bit downhearted.

*   *   *   *   *

"Guess what?" Brenda greeted Bobby when he got home. "Sonny's mother called and told Mama that she found a nursing home in Connecticut that had a Mrs. Griffin registered."

"Thanks, Brenda," Mrs. Thompson said, a frown on her face. "Girl, if you don't stop listening to my conversations…Mrs. Henderson said she found three nursing homes in Connecticut with a Mrs. Griffin registered," Mrs. Thompson corrected.

Bobby's spirits suddenly soared. Apparently Sonny's did too, because just as Bobby opened the door to race down to Sonny's, his friend was about to knock.

"Did you hear? Mrs. Griffin is in a nursing home in Connecticut," Bobby announced.

"Not one, three. Mama said three. Here's the names. She wrote them on this piece of paper." Sonny handed Bobby a small scrap of paper on which was written the names of the nursing homes, Whippoorwill Rest Home, Sunnyvale Meadows, and Longfield Convalescent Home, all in Hartford.

"Could we go, Mama, please!" Bobby pleaded.

"Take it easy, boys. You're both too young to go traipsing all over Connecticut by yourselves. Besides, what will you do if you find her?"

"Can't you or Daddy come with us?"

"Tomorrow I have to work at the beauty shop all day. Your daddy won't be home until late either."

"What about Mr. Williams. Can we ask him?" Sonny asked.

"Well, I don't know anything about this Mr. Williams. In the meantime, I'll have to speak with your mother, Sonny. And Bobby, Daddy and I'll talk it over tonight."

That evening Mrs. Thompson talked not only to Charlotte and Mr. Thompson, but she called Mr. Williams as well. Finally, they all agreed to let the boys go as long as Mr. Williams accompanied them.

Chapter Ten

The next morning, Bobby awoke early. It had rained the night before, but the November day, though around fifty degrees, was clear. Dressed in corduroys and his thick jacket with a hood, he hurried down to his friend's apartment. Sonny, too, wore a heavy jacket and cap. Around his neck was a colorful scarf Charlotte had crocheted. They had agreed to meet Mr. Williams in front of his apartment at 10 a.m. Mr. Williams was anxious himself; however, he cautioned the boys not to get their hopes up.

"If we find Mrs. Griffin, she may not be in any condition to come home. We'll just wait and see."

The ride to Hartford, Connecticut seemed long. Bobby watched the landscape change from tall buildings to single-family houses and more greenery—trees, bushes, and wide-open spaces where the children beyond the bus window lived in a world far different from his. Bobby tried to imagine what a typical day living there would be like. Not having gotten much sleep the night before, Sonny dozed while Mr. Williams, sat quietly, lost in his memories as the miles sped by.

Finally they arrived in Hartford. As the bus wound its way through the city, Bobby felt his anxiety grow. Suppose it was another Mrs. Griffin, not the one he knew, but a different person with the same name? If it was Mrs. Griffin, suppose she was seriously ill and couldn't come home? At least, he reasoned, they'd know where she was and that was better than the way it was now. The bus pulled into the depot and the three of them got off.

"Which one should we check first?" Bobby asked. They went up to the information booth and spoke with the clerk, a stout white man about ten years younger than Mr. Williams, his bald head almost obscured by a visor. His generous stomach kept him from sitting too close to the counter. From him, they learned that Whippoorwill Rest Home was on the edge of the city in an exclusive area surrounded by wealthy homes.

"Do you think Mrs. Griffin could be there?" asked Sonny.

"I doubt it. I mean, she's not exactly poor, but she's not rich either," Mr. Williams responded. "How far is Longfield Convalescent Hospital?"

The clerk gave them directions. It was within walking distance from the bus depot.

"What about Sunnyvale Meadows? How far away is that?" Bobby asked the clerk.

"Way over on the other side of town," the clerk answered. "You gotta take a taxi to reach it."

"First we'll check out Longfield Convalescent; then we'll go over to Sunnyvale," Mr. Williams said.

It took them over a half hour to locate Longfield Convalescent Hospital and then another thirty minutes to learn that no one by the name of Ida Mae Griffin was registered.

"Can we stop and get something to eat? I'm starving," Sonny asked.

"Me, too," Bobby agreed.

"I believe I could use a bite, too," said Mr. Williams. They located the nearest White Castle and put away enough hamburgers, fries and soda to hold them until they returned home. Then they set out for the last place on their list.

Forty minutes later their taxi stopped in front of a dilapidated house with the words "Sunnyvale Meadows" on an unpainted sign in front. The neighborhood looked worse than any street Bobby had seen in Harlem. As he glanced about, he shivered. Run-down two-story row houses flanked the street. Cracks in the sidewalk made walking hazardous. Even though garbage cans stood beside each building, rubbish was everywhere except in them. Though it was Sunday, the streets were teeming with adults and children. The children's screams along with the music blaring from radios created an atmosphere of chaos.

Several pairs of eyes followed the trio as they walked up the stairs. Mr. Williams knocked on the screen door. On the porch sat two old people in wheel chairs, one staring vacantly at the ground, the other carrying on an animated conversation with no one in particular. As they waited for someone to come to the door, their noses were assaulted by the worse imaginable smells—of urine, disinfectant, vomit, and neglect. Sonny sneezed. Just inside, Bobby could see several other people sitting in chairs opposite the door, but no one made a move to answer their knock.

Finally, a big woman in a white uniform sauntered lazily to the door. She was carrying a cup of hot coffee which she sipped as she walked.

"You folks come to visit a relative?" She smiled sweetly through the screen. "I wish you had called first. We don't get many visitors and we get upset when people drop in un-expectantly, don't we?" She made no move to let them in.

Mr. Williams explained their purpose. Nurse Foster, as she introduced herself, opened the door and ushered them into the living room.

"She's been feeling poorly lately. Not up to her cheerful self," Nurse Foster explained happily. "You all just make yourselves comfortable, and don't pay no attention to my babies." She gestured to three elderly women and one man who stared expectantly at the visitors. "They get so excited when company comes."

Though she spoke in a friendly manner, the boys were overwhelmed by her size. Weighing over 250 pounds and close to 6 feet tall, Nurse Foster was an impressive figure. Beneath her seemingly pleasant demeanor, however, Sonny sensed a wariness. She told them to have a seat while she went to check to see if Mrs. Griffin was up to seeing visitors.

The room with several straight back chairs, an old Victorian sofa, and a wooden table that stood against the wall was dark and oppressive. The only light came from a gap in the heavily curtained window. Bobby led Sonny to one of the straight back chairs, and he sat down in the other. Mr. Williams sat on the sofa.

As they waited, one of the women came over and sat near them. She appeared to be in her seventies with short white hair and thin, wrinkled skin. Her gnarled fingers clutched her purse close to her body as if guarding precious jewels. Freeing one hand, she stroked Bobby's hair.

"When my son was your age, he liked to wear his hair long." She laughed. "Wouldn't let me get near it with a comb. Cared more about his hair than he did me or anybody else. Hah! Now he's bald. Serves him right. Ain't got nothing up top." Her laughter sent chills down Bobby's spine and he wished Nurse Foster would hurry back.

Another woman rolled into the room, her legs propelling the wheel-chair expertly towards them. Around her torso were strips of cloth tying her firmly to the chair.

"Will you untie these for me?" she asked Mr. Williams. "They put these on me to keep me from falling out of this chair, but now I got to go to the bathroom and there ain't nobody around."

Mr. Williams reached around for one of the knots.

"Don't do it!" the old gentleman sitting across from them spoke abruptly. "Sophie, you know they got you tied up for a reason. You always trying to run away and then, where you gonna go?"

A cigarette dangled from the side of his mouth, the ashes scattered down the front of his faded suit jacket, a jacket that seemed much too large for his bony frame. His legs were crossed at the knee. The top one swung steadily keeping time to some imaginary beat.

"She does that with everybody who comes here. Always asking them to untie her and they always do unless somebody stops them," the woman with the purse added.

"One time she got away and almost got as far as the corner before they could catch her," the old gentleman said.

Nurse Foster strolled leisurely back to their relief. The cup still in one hand, a cigarette in the other.

"Sorry, Mrs. Griffin can't see anybody today. Like I said before, she's feeling under the weather."

"But can't we see her just for a minute?" Sonny asked.

"We not gonna stay long. We just wanta make sure it's Mrs. Ida Mae Griffin," said Bobby.

"Are you relatives?" Nurse Foster asked, suspicion clouding her eyes.

"No…" Bobby was about to say.

"Yes," Mr. Williams broke in. "These are her great nephews and I promised them I'd bring them to see their aunt."

Nurse Foster eyed them closely before she spoke. "The director said Mrs. Griffin couldn't have no visitors, relatives or not."

"Not even for a moment?" Sonny asked.

"I'm sorry. No visitors! Now if you'll just follow me, I'll let you out."

"Wait a minute," Mr. Williams said, his voice rising. "Let me talk to the director. We came all the way from New York City and you're telling us we can't see Mrs. Griffin? What kind of place is this?"

"The director is not here today. If you'll call tomorrow…"

"I will *not* call tomorrow! I want to see Mrs. Griffin *Now!*" Mr. Williams was angry. Bobby could see him shaking behind his glasses.

"Who do you think you're talking to?" Nurse Foster's anger too seemed to rise up out of nowhere and threatened to overwhelm everybody. "*If you don't get out of here now, I'll call the police!*"

Just as suddenly, the mood in the place changed from calm indifference to curious tension. Everyone's eyes were on them. Several of the mobile patients started for the door. Others turned their wheelchairs towards the trio and waited in anticipation.

"Oh Lord, there's gonna be a fight," the old gentleman said, breaking the silence.

"I gotta get out of here. Somebody please help me!" one of the women yelled.

The elderly man tried to get up out of his chair, but he couldn't quite get his feet to cooperate. The woman who was tied to the chair laughed hysterically. Bobby tugged at Mr. Williams's arm. Sonny and Bobby managed to get him to the porch, down the stairs, and around the block before he calmed down.

"I'm sorry, fellows," Mr. Williams said when his anger had abated. "I didn't mean to make a fool of myself. It's just that places like that scare me. And to think that Ida Mae is in there, I just don't know." He shook his head. "One thing I do know is that woman's not gonna let us back in there. That's for sure."

They sat down on a nearby bench, heads down, not voicing their thoughts.

"There's got to be a way to get in there," Sonny said.

Suddenly, turning to Sonny, Bobby said, "Remember how we slipped in to see your mother when she was in the hospital last year?"

Sonny's face lit up with the memory of them slipping past the desk and guard to visit her when she had broken her leg. "Yeah. I remember. But how do we get past Nurse Foster?"

"I don't know, boys," Mr. Williams said. "And seeing as how I'm responsible for you, I don't want no trouble. Maybe we should get hold of the authorities and let them handle it."

"But we still don't know for sure if it is our Mrs. Griffin in there. It could be somebody else," Sonny said.

"You're right, Sonny," Mr. Williams rubbed his temples. "But how?"

"I'll find out. You wait here." Bobby was half way down the block before they could stop him.

*   *   *   *

While Mr. Williams and Sonny waited, Bobby went back to the house and circled around to the rear. He came upon a little fenced-in yard filled with an assortment of discarded items, bottles, rusted cans, tires scattered here and there, and in one far corner, turned on its side, a weather-beaten chair. He found a place in the chain-linked fence through which he crawled. The back door was unlocked. Cautiously, he opened the door and climbed the squeaky stairs to the second floor. Along the corridor he saw doors, some open, some closed. Sounds of someone moaning came from behind one door. Bobby peeked in. Lying on a small bed, covered from the neck down, was a man. He moaned as if in tremendous pain. Bobby quickly shut the door. He approached another door and looked in. A figure lay in the bed covered from head to toe, like the man in the room he had just visited. All that showed was the top of a head. Bobby crept up to the bed and peered down at the sleeping figure. Her back was to him.

"Mrs. Griffin," he whispered as he reached out to touch her. "Mrs. Griffin," he repeated. Slowly the woman turned over. Her eyes opened slowly, glazed and unfocussed, a faraway look in them as they circled the room coming to rest on Bobby's face.

"Mrs. Griffin. It's me, Bobby." His heart pounded.

"Bobby? Is it really you?" A smile spread across her face as she tried to lift her head.

"So! I thought I heard somebody up here." Bobby heard a gruff voice behind him. "You come with me." Nurse Foster grabbed him by his collar and hauled him from the room. Though he struggled to free himself from her grasp, he couldn't. She was just about to toss him out the door when a woman walked in.

She was dressed in a dark business suit, and carried a briefcase. With her pale skin, her hair pulled back into a tight bun and glasses perched on the end of her nose, she reminded Bobby of his English teacher, Miss Lester. Immediately, Nurse Foster released him and he fell to the floor.

"What's going on here?" the woman asked in an authoritative tone.

"Dr. Alexander, I caught this boy upstairs in one of the rooms disturbing one of our patients."

"I wasn't," Bobby yelled, rubbing his sore neck. "You got Mrs. Griffin locked up."

"Son, nobody is kept here against their will. This is a nursing home, not a prison."

"Then how come you won't let nobody see her?"

"I told him she was asleep and couldn't be disturbed," Nurse Foster explained. "I told his friends the same thing, but then they got the other patients upset and…."

"Thank you, Foster," Dr. Alexander broke in. "That will be all, nurse. I'll handle this young man's problem."

Dr. Alexander dismissed the nurse and indicated that Bobby should follow her to her office. As they started down the hall, Mr. Williams and Sonny who had been standing just outside, entered. They fell in step behind Bobby.

Once inside the large office which looked out on a small well-kept garden surrounded by a wall that made one forget the blighted community behind it, they were seated. Bobby glanced around the room noticing the certificates on the wall, the photograph of a family—husband, wife and two children—on the desk. The woman in the photograph was Dr. Alexander minus the bun, business suit and glasses. In the photo she looked a lot younger.

"My sanctuary," she said, her voice now soft and friendly. "I apologize for the appearance of this place. It's really not as bad as it looks. Seldom do we have visitors. Actually, we try to make our residents feel as much at home as possible." Seeing the grimace on Mr. Williams's face, her voice trailed off. A look of exasperation replaced the professional smile. "Too many people put their relatives in nursing homes because they can't or don't want to deal with them anymore. For many here, this is their last home, and with too little money and lack of adequate staff, we do the best we can."

The doctor explained that Mrs. Griffin had been brought to the home by her niece and signed in. "Her niece, Mrs. Hopkins, said she was no longer able to care for her aunt and she felt her aunt was unable to live alone, being a danger to herself and others. When she was brought in, she was in a highly emotional state and had to be sedated.

"Since she's been here she has refused to eat and on several occasions has tried to run away. What's more, Mrs. Hopkins left specific instructions that she was not to receive any visitors because it would upset her further."

Mr. Williams explained everything to Dr. Alexander, who listened silently until he finished. After some moments, she spoke.

"I'm afraid there is nothing I can do. I can't release her to you because you are not related. Mrs. Hopkins is the only one who can sign her out."

"What about Mrs. Griffin? Can't she sign herself out?" Sonny asked.

"No, she can't." Dr. Alexander glanced at her watch. "I will allow you to see her, but only for a few minutes though it's against our policy to go against a relative's instructions. However, under the circumstances…"

Bobby leaped to his feet and started for the door before the others moved.

Mr. Williams apologized for the commotion caused by their arrival. As he and Dr. Alexander shook hands, the boys started up the stairs to Mrs. Griffin's room.

Chapter Eleven

"*I* can't believe it's you. I thought I'd never see you all again." Mrs. Griffin hugged Bobby and Sonny so tightly, Bobby felt he'd lose his breath.

When she saw Mr. Williams, she held out her hands and he took them, his eyes moist with tears. For a while they sat looking at each other without speaking. Bobby and Sonny waited, feeling awkward.

Though she looked frail and slightly disoriented, her mind was sharp. Disappointment briefly shadowed her face when they told her they couldn't sign her out. Only her niece could do that.

"But I don't have a niece!" Her voice, at first a whisper, gathered strength as she spoke. "As far as I know, my brother was never married."

"Then who brought you here?" Sonny asked.

"I don't suppose you remember a few months ago, a young couple moved into the building. The woman, Florence Hopkins, and I became very friendly. She visited me often and sometimes we went shopping together. Then, quite suddenly, she and her husband moved out. I hadn't seen or spoken to her for over a month. Late one evening, I think it was the last time we were together when I promised I'd tell you about Marcus Garvey?"

"And you promised to make us a apple pie?" Bobby interrupted.

"That's right," Mrs. Griffin smiled. "When you left, Florence and her husband came by. I told them I was on my way to bed, but they insisted they had to talk to me about something important. Florence brought me a glass of warm milk while she and her husband Dwight had some wine, you know, the bottle I keep for special occasions." She glanced over at Mr. Williams who smiled and nodded. "We had just sat down to talk and the next thing I knew, I was here."

"What did they want to talk to you about? Do you remember?" asked Mr. Williams.

"They wanted me to sign some papers. I don't know what for? All I remember is that I suddenly felt extremely drowsy. I must have fallen asleep. When I woke up, as I said, I was in here. Nobody would tell me anything."

"There's got to be a way to get her out of here," Sonny said to Bobby just as Nurse Foster appeared at the door.

"Your time is up!" she said harshly.

"Give us just a few more minutes, please," Mrs. Griffin pleaded, her eyes scanning the nurse's hard face. The woman's face softened.

"I'll give you two more minutes; then your visitors have got to leave."

When she'd gone, the four of them tried to think of ways to get her released. Unfortunately, all paths led back to Florence Hopkins. Without her, even with a lawyer to prove Mrs. Griffin was kidnapped and placed in the nursing home against her will, it would take too long, maybe months. Finding Florence Hopkins was the key. But where she was and why she signed Mrs. Griffin into the home remained a question.

One thing for sure, Bobby and Sonny vowed they'd find her with Mr. Williams's help and get Mrs. Griffin released. As they rode the bus back to Harlem, they all felt as if a weight had been lifted from their shoulders.

*   *   *   *

Thanksgiving was celebrated at the Thompson's. Both Charlotte and Sonny were invited to share in the feast along with Mr. Williams. Bobby and Brenda were assigned to clean up the bathroom and straighten up the living room while Mrs. Thompson shopped and cooked. Mr. Thompson helped wherever he was needed to lift this and move that. Charlotte brought collard greens and candied yams. Mr. Williams brought mincemeat pie. Still, despite the happy gathering, Mrs. Griffin's absence hung in the air like fog. It lifted somewhat when Mrs.

Thompson announced she would fix a plate to take to Mrs. Griffin the next day.

Finding Florence Hopkins was not going to be an easy feat. The boys didn't know where to start. Two weeks passed and they still had no clues as to her whereabouts. Every chance they got, they rode along with Mr. Williams to visit Mrs. Griffin. Though she was always happy to see them, her smile was tinged with sadness. Because they had no good news to bring her, there was always a cloud hanging over their visits. When they came, they always brought her mail and reassured her that her cat, King Tut, was being well cared for at Sonny's. Still nothing would have cheered her better than the news that Florence Hopkins had been found.

One day they brought her a batch of letters.

"What's this?" she said as she tore open an official looking letter and handed it to Bobby to read since she had been unable to find her reading glasses.

"It's from the Circuit Court of Halifax County, Virginia," Bobby said.

"Why would the Circuit Court be writing me?"

"The purpose of this suit is to as...aser..." Bobby handed the document over to Mr. Williams. He reached into his pocket and carefully removed his reading glasses from its case. Slowly placing them on his face, he adjusted them over each ear and pushed them up over the bridge of his nose. He cleared his throat and read,

The purpose of this suit is to ascertain the ownership of the land located in Roanoke District of Halifax County, Virginia...containing 100 acres.

Mr. Williams whistled.

"Is that a lot of land?" asked Bobby.

"Sounds like," added Sonny.

An affidavit having been made and filed that the following defendant, Ida Mae Griffin, of New York, must appear on or before December 13 and do what may be necessary to protect her interests here..."

"Two weeks from today," Mr. Williams looked up from the letter.

"What do it mean?" Bobby asked.

"I thought you sold all your land, Ida Mae," Mr. Williams said, folding up the document and handing it back to Bobby who placed it back in the envelope.

"I did. What they're talking about must be some land my grandparents owned."

"Somebody must want to buy it. All living relatives have to be notified before they can sell it," said Mr. Williams.

"What happens if you don't answer. Can they sell it anyway?" Sonny asked.

"I'm not sure. At any rate, there's not much I can do in here?"

"I wonder if there's a connection between you being in here and the Hopkins." Sonny asked, wheels beginning to spin in his head. "Did Miss Florence ever say where she lived before she came to New York?"

"Why, I think she did. I believe she mentioned Virginia. But she's not a relative, so I don't see how this has anything to do with her."

"It would be a motive," said Bobby his detective juices flowing.

*　　　　*　　　　*　　　　*

As soon as they arrived back on the block, Bobby ran upstairs to tell his folks he was home. Then he hurried down to Sonny's.

"We've gotta go back to Tiny's."

"But they wouldn't tell us anything the last time we were there," Sonny protested.

"We gotta try again."

*　　　　*　　　　*　　　　*

The next morning, instead of going to school, both decided to go over to Tiny's Haven. Sonny convinced his mother he wasn't feeling well. Mrs. Henderson took his temperature which was normal, checked his pulse, and shook her head.

"Stay in bed, keep warm and call me if you need me. There's a virus going round and it's better to be safe than sorry." She kissed him on the forehead and left for work.

When Bobby told his parents he was ill, his father said, "Boy, you'd better get up out of that bed. You're just trying to get out of going to school."

Bobby coughed several times loudly, holding his chest and tried to look as miserable as he could.

"Now Joe," Mrs. Thompson said. "Bobby doesn't usually get sick, but if he is, I'd rather he stay home than spread whatever he has around to the other children."

Reluctantly Mr. Thompson consented. Mrs. Thompson made Bobby swallow a teaspoon of Castor Oil and rubbed his chest down with Vicks Salve. Then, both parents left for work. Bobby waited for Brenda to leave before jumping out of bed. He washed off the Vicks, brushed his teeth and his tongue, and rinsed his mouth out with his father's Listerine to get rid of the oily taste. As soon as he had eaten cereal and drunk a glass of orange juice, he rushed down to Sonny's. They knew they'd be in trouble when their parents found out about their deception, but, as Bobby reasoned, it was for a good cause, especially if they found Florence and were able to get Mrs. Griffin released.

Because it was so early in the morning, the club was not open and according to the sign on the door, was not expected to open until 11 a.m. It had begun to drizzle and a chill filled the wintry air. Though they had dressed warmly, it wasn't long before they began to wonder if they'd truly get sick. Just as they settled down for the three-hour wait, a car drove up and a man got out. He was a small man in his early fifties, with a thick salt and pepper mustache and a slight limp for which he carried a cane. He walked up to the door, keys in hand.

"Shouldn't you boys be in school?" he said, eyeing them closely. His husky voice was warm and friendly, giving Bobby the courage he needed to answer.

"We was waiting for the owner."

"What do you want to see the owner about? You're too young to be looking for a job?"

After Sonny explained the situation, Mr. Harris, who happened to be the owner of Tiny's, shook his head sympathetically.

"That is a sad situation. Sorry, the Dwight Hopkins Trio finished their gig a couple of nights ago and moved on. But I'll see if I can find the information you need. He glanced up at the sky, "It looks like it might snow. You all had better come inside."

Mr. Harris invited the boys to wait just inside while he went to his office to look up his records. He disappeared down the dimly lit hallway. Once again Bobby glanced around the quiet room. Stale smoke hovered in the air like clouds and mingled with the smell of beer, alcohol and sweat. He imagined what the club looked like in the evenings crowded with people.

"Where's the piano?" Sonny suddenly asked after Bobby described the decor.

"On the left side of the stage. It's much bigger than Mrs. Griffin's."

"Sure wish I could play it. I haven't practiced since she went away. Do you think Mr. Harris would mind if I touched it?"

"I don't know. I guess it wouldn't hurt." Bobby led Sonny over to the bandstand and sat him at the piano. "Hurry up, though."

Sonny spread his fingers across the keys and began to play "Mood Indigo," softly.

"Say kid, where did you learn to play like that? You got a good touch," Mr. Harris said, sitting down beside Sonny and picking up in the middle of the piece. He finished it and went on to play several more tunes as he talked.

"I don't play much anymore, too busy." His style reminded Sonny of Art Tatum, one of his idols. To Sonny, of all the jazz pianist he'd ever head, Art Tatum was the best.

When he had finished, Mr. Harris handed them a slip of paper. "This is all I could find. Musicians don't usually stay any place for long. Hope you can locate him and get everything squared away."

He shook both boys' hands and patted Sonny on the back.

"Come back when you're a little older and you got a job."

Though the cold air greeted them, the sun had emerged from the clouds and the rain had stopped. Their spirits buoyed, the boys felt that at last they had a concrete lead.

"It ain't too far from here. 116th street and Morningside Avenue," Bobby said. "I got my fingers and toes crossed."

The boys hurried down the long blocks to 116th street passing street-sweeping trucks washing down gutters. Pedestrians scrambled to the side of the nearest buildings to keep from getting sprayed. Postal workers carried large sacks of mail. Delivery trucks delivered goods and produce to the small grocery stores and restaurants that dotted the busy street. They passed sanitation workers picking up last nights trash, and small storeowners sweeping down their entranceways.

Finally they stopped in front of a tenement that looked like most of the other apartment buildings in Harlem, closely built six story structures with a multitude of windows that peered curiously out at the streets below. Since it was still early, few people sat at those windows or on the stoops.

Bobby felt an attack of nerves. He could tell by the pressure of Sonny's fingers on his arm that he, too, was anxious. Bobby read the names on the mailboxes, but unfortunately, the names Dwight or Florence Hopkins was not among them.

"What we gonna do now?" Bobby asked, trying to hold down his disappointment.

"We could come back or wait, but we don't know for sure they're still living here. Maybe we could talk to the manager."

Bobby spotted a small sign in the corner of a window that read, "Apartment for Rent. See manager in Apartment 1A."

The manager's apartment was behind the staircase. Bobby listened for a moment before knocking. Inside he heard the sounds of a television and little children running up and down. After a few minutes, the door opened and a woman holding a baby stood there. A scowl on her face, she looked them up and down.

"You selling something, because I don't allow no selling in this building." The woman started to close the door.

"Could you tell us if Dwight Hopkins live here?" Bobby asked, nervously.

"He's a musician, plays the trumpet," Sonny added.

"Ain't no musicians living here. Now, I'm busy. I don't have no time to be answering questions."

Behind her came a loud crash followed by arguing. Yelling over her shoulder, "Amanda, how many times I gotta tell you…!" she rushed inside, the baby bouncing up and down on her hip.

The boys waited for her return. Just inside Bobby saw a little girl run across the room crying. The woman returned to the door.

She eyed them suspiciously, "Why do want to know?"

"We need to get in touch with them," Sonny said. "It's a matter of life and death."

"Yeah, life and death," Bobby echoed.

Reluctantly, the woman told them a young couple did move in.

"But, the man moved out shortly after. I don't know whether he was a musician. Never heard him playing no music and I don't get into my tenants' business."

"You said the man moved out. What about the woman, Florence Hopkins? Do she still live here?" Bobby asked.

"Yeah, at least I saw her go out this morning? Say, why ain't you boys in school. Is this a holiday or something?"

"Do you know what time she comes home?" Sonny asked.

"Frankie! I told you to put that down!" The woman ran into the apartment again. This time she slammed the door behind her. Loud wailing and feet scurrying issued from inside.

"So, Miss Florence still lives here. I wonder what apartment? We should'da asked," Bobby said as they prepared for a long wait.

By 2 o'clock, they were tired and restless sitting on the hard concrete steps with empty stomachs. Luckily the temperature had climbed from where it was in the morning, the air no longer chilled. Few people entered or left the building. Bobby and Sonny pooled what little money they had and Bobby went to the store returning with two bags of potato chips, two candy bars, and two cans of soda. By four o'clock they began to worry about what they had done and what their parents would say when they learned of it.

"Maybe we'd better go home and come back later," Sonny suggested.

"If we leave now, we might miss her and Mrs. Griffin won't never get out of the hospital and she'll lose all her property."

At 5:30 just as they were about to give up, they spotted a thin woman coming towards them. Her eyes averted, she didn't see them until she was right up on them. When she did, she jumped.

"Mrs. Hopkins? Are you Florence Hopkins?" Bobby asked standing up, blocking the stairs.

The woman, slightly taller than Bobby, looked tired and frail, too thin for her height. She couldn't have been as old as his mother, Bobby thought. Maybe in her twenties and despite the dark shadows beneath her eyes, she was almost pretty. She reached up and touched her short hair self consciously as she avoided Bobby's eyes.

"No, I d' don't know who you're t'talking about," she said quickly sidestepping him.

Something in her manner made Bobby press the matter.

"Please, it's about Mrs. Griffin," he said following after her.

She stopped and turned towards him looking at him for the first time.

"I don't know no Mrs. Griffin," she said, a voice a little more than a whisper. "You b' boys better get out of here before I call the ca cops."

"She's Florence Hopkins. I know she is!" said Sonny remembering how Mrs. Griffin had described her, her slight stutter.

"Mrs. Hopkins, we come to ask you to sign some papers to let Mrs. Griffin out of the nursing home you put her in." Bobby pressed on. As Florence dashed up the stairs, they followed. She ran up the five flights of stairs, down the hall and tried to unlock the door and rush in; however, Bobby was too quick. As she tried to shut the door, he squeezed his foot in and kept it open long enough for Sonny to catch up. Florence collapsed on the couch, her hands covering her face. She let out a loud moan.

"I knew it! I knew they'd find out." She looked up at them through a tear-streaked face. "I knew we sh shouldn't have done it. I told D'Dwight it wasn't right."

The boys didn't have to ask her anything. She seemed to want to talk. She told them that Dwight had thought up the scheme saying it would-n't hurt anybody. That once they had the money, they'd have Mrs. Griffin released.

"Dwight left me two w weeks ago. I ain't seen him since. Once the papers were f filed, he disappeared without a w word. Is Mrs. Griffin all right? I didn't mean her no harm."

"What papers?" Sonny asked. "The hearing is not until the thirteenth."

"I found out that Dwight was working with these group of men that buy land. They wanted us to get Mrs. Griffin to sign over her property to them. Dwight thought up the scheme to have her put in a nursing home."

"How could he sell what he don't own?" Sonny asked.

"He had Mrs. Griffin's power of attorney," Florence answered. "She didn't k know what she was s signing. I had put sleeping m medicine in her milk and she was groggy."

"But Mrs. Griffin just got a letter from the court," Bobby said.

"I don't know nothing about that. All I know is that once they paid him, he left. He had what he wanted, and he took off without a word." Her tone grew bitter.

The boys stayed a while longer. Florence talked about her and Dwight's relationship seemingly oblivious of the boys' presence. In the end, she agreed to go the first thing in the morning to sign Mrs. Griffin's release.

On the way home with feelings of satisfaction, the boys discussed their next move.

"What day is it?" Sonny asked, suddenly.

"Tuesday, I think," said Bobby.

"No, I mean the date. What is today's date?"

"I don't know. I think it's the 10th."

"And if Mrs. Griffin doesn't get there, she'll lose everything! The hearing is on the thirteenth. That means we got three days to get her out of the nursing home so that she can go to Virginia to that hearing!" said Sonny his voice filled with anxiety.

Chapter Twelve

"*H*ummm, this sure is good pie," Bobby said starting on his third piece.

"Can I have another piece?" Sonny asked. "This is the best apple I ever tasted!"

"Sure is the best one I've had in a long time," Mr. Williams said, wiping his lips.

Mrs. Griffin laughed as she and Brenda brought in glasses of milk and set them down on the table. As a surprise homecoming, Mrs. Thompson, Charlotte Henderson, and several other neighbors got together and decorated Mrs. Griffin's apartment for Christmas. A tiny tree festooned with blinking light bulbs and colorful ornaments stood on the side table. A wreath hung on the door. A miniature Nativity scene sat on top of the piano. The holiday decorations gave her small apartment a festive atmosphere. Outside the first snow of the season began to fall.

"I don't know where I'd be if it wasn't for you all. It's a blessing to be loved. Everything turned out as it should."

"But why didn't you keep the land, Mrs. Griffin?" Mr. Thompson asked. "From what I've read, land is very valuable."

"I didn't sell it. I leased it to my neighbor. He's a part of an organization that is trying to keep black folk from selling their land."

"What about Florence Hopkins. Was she really your niece?" asked Sonny's mother.

"Not really. She claimed that my brother was her father. Actually, she was the daughter of my brother's wife by her first marriage. She was never adopted because my brother died before he had time to arrange to adopt her. I guess she didn't find out until recently."

"What's gonna happen to her?" Brenda asked.

"I don't know. I feel sorry for her. Searched all her life for love and when she thought she'd found somebody, turns out he was just using her."

"If she hadn't worked for that family, she'd never know about Mrs. Griffin's land and…"

"And none of this would have happened," said Charlotte.

"And we wouldn't be here eating Mrs. Griffin's pie either," Mrs. Thompson added.

"Now we'd better be getting home and give Mrs. Griffin a chance to catch up on everything. Finish your plates. Brenda and I'll wash up." She piled the empty dishes on the tray and carried them into the kitchen.

"Do you think they'll ever find Dwight Hopkins?" Sonny asked.

"Naw," said Mr. Williams. "I doubt it. If they do, I hope I get first chance at him."

They all laughed as Mr. Williams made a gesture of a boxer throwing an uppercut.

"That reminds me of Joe Lewis. I know you all are too young to remember the Brown Bomber*," said Mrs. Griffin.

---

* *Joseph Louis Barrow (1914–1981) known as the Brown Bomber, held the World Heavyweight Championship title for almost twelve years, the longest reign in the history of the heavyweight division.*

The Intruder

Chapter One

Sonny heard voices coming through the radiator pipes, loud angry voices. He moved closer to listen.

"What'd I tell you about messing with my stuff?"

"Jim, I ain't moved nothing. Last time I saw your shirt, it was laying over that chair. If you'd hang your clothes up, you'd know right where they is!"

"Don't talk to me like I'm some kind of child. Just find me my blue shirt."

"Why can't you wear this plaid one? It's clean and pressed."

"Cause I want my blue one, that's why."

Charlotte Henderson strode into Sonny's room and kissed him on the cheek. "Now you be good. I'll be home, hopefully, by five. You know where you can reach me if you need to." Though dressed in her starched nurse's uniform, she felt warm and soft to Sonny. His nose twitched as he took in the faint spicy smell of her favorite perfume. He hugged her and listened as she left the apartment for Harlem Hospital where she worked as a Licensed Vocational Nurse.

A short while later, he heard a door slam and footsteps descending hurriedly. Mr. Washington was on his way to work. It was spring and for one week, school was out. Sonny felt Sheba rub against his leg. He reached down, picked the kitten up and stroked her soft fur. The youngest of the litter, Sheba was a gift from Mrs. Griffin for taking care of her Abyssinian cat, King Tut. The neighborhood mentor, Mrs. Griffin nurtured the children of the community. She taught them about their cultural heritage and proper social graces, and encouraged them to develop their natural gifts. Just a few months earlier, Bobby and Sonny helped get her released from a nursing home in time to save her property.

"What are we going to do today?" Sonny spoke gently to the kitten. "I'd better get dressed before Bobby comes. But first, let's eat breakfast. Are you hungry?" Frisky and playful, Sheba leaped from his arms and dashed under the bed.

Sonny, who was eleven-years old, was visually handicapped. He'd lost his sight to glaucoma when he was four. He was a little taller than his friend Bobby, with skinny arms and long legs, all skin and bones, his mother described him. His complexion was the color of honey. Freckles were scattered along his nose. Unlike Bobby whose head was crowned in a thick mass of black hair, Sonny's hair was a fine and curly, medium brown tinged with red in the sunlight. A bright young man, Sonny was quiet, thoughtful, and a bit shy. Knowing Bobby had brought out another side to his personality, a desire for adventure.

Suddenly he heard a familiar knock. Two slow raps followed by two rapid ones. He hastened over to the radiator to reply. It was their signal. It meant Bobby was up and ready to start the day. He quickly dressed in his jeans and tee shirt and sat down to eat his breakfast, Cheerios and milk. While he waited for Bobby, he decided to listen to his jazz records. Thanks to his mother, Sonny had an extensive and valuable record collection, not only of jazz, but classical and the latest hits by Little Stevie Wonder, the Jackson Five and Marvin Gaye. Each record was carefully labeled in Braille and arranged in neat rows so that Sonny could easily locate whichever one he wanted to listen to. He and his mother had set up a system over many weekends and evenings. The same system worked with all his books. Charlotte tried to provide her eleven year old with whatever she thought would satisfy his curious mind. Before he met Bobby, his world evolved around his room and the things his mother provided to keep him safe. Years ago, a prank involving boys from his old neighborhood in Cleveland had traumatized him and prompted his mother to take drastic measures to safeguard her son.

Rap, Rap, rap, rap. Two long and two short raps sounded on the front door. Bobby bounded into Apartment 2C as he entered wherever he went. The same age as Sonny, Bobby Thompson was just under 5 ft. tall, active and outgoing. Dark chocolate complexion and deep dimples like his father, he had a thick mass of hair which his mother constantly nagged him about combing. He seemed to have limitless energy. Outgoing, curious, with a highly developed imagination, Bobby was always ready to take on a new adventure. He and Sonny were opposites which made their friendship special. Whereas school came easy for Sonny, for Bobby it was a struggle.

"Hey, Brenda made some cookies last night. They taste horrible. Do you want one?" Bobby produced a bag filled with small lumpy cookies and placed one in Sonny's hand.

"What kind are they?" Sonny asked.

"Who knows. I think she put everything she could find in them, raisins, peanut butter, nuts, and oatmeal. They ain't so bad. Just hard as rocks."

"Well, what are we going to do today? Whatever it is, I'm ready," Sonny said, eager to get started. A week went by too quickly.

"Let's go over to the park."

The boys made their way down to the street and squeezed past the women who sat like sentries blocking the entranceway to their fortress. Instead of their usual inquiries, the two women seemed preoccupied, almost too preoccupied to notice them. Snatches of their conversation reached the boys' ears.

"Something's going on. I don't know what it is but something ain't right," Mrs. Mobley said as she massaged the bunion on her right foot. A large, buxom woman in her late fifties, Mrs. Mobley was almost as wide as she was short. Her hair was always in rollers hidden beneath a scarf. She wore an apron over a cotton housedress and house slippers. Seldom did she or Mrs. Vincent leave their post guarding the entranceway to the building except long after dark or if the weather was bad.

"Nothing's ever right with you. You're always looking for trouble even when there ain't none around," said Mrs. Vincent. Unlike Mrs. Mobley, Mrs. Vincent was skinny and reminded Bobby of a scarecrow he'd seen on TV. Her voice was high and scratchy. In her early sixties as well, she wore a housedress, socks around her skinny ankles, and slippers. Both wore thick sweaters to protect them from the chilly wind.

"I tell you, something's going on. Don't believe me until it's too late. Then we'll see."

"Wonder what they talking about?" Bobby asked after they had gone a few yards from the building.

"Wish I knew." They walked past the corner store and up the hill towards Colonial Park.

The park sprawled across several city blocks forming an oasis from the surrounding concrete buildings. It housed the public swimming pool, the main attraction for young and old during the summer. Wooden benches flanked the path that meandered throughout several areas of the park. In one area sat concrete picnic tables where men gathered to play board games. In another area swings, monkey bars, and a seesaw for children stood. A short distance away was a sandbox for the very young. There was an area of benches where drummers and other musicians gathered. All along the perimeter were tall trees that hid the view of the surrounding buildings and deadened the sounds of the constantly moving traffic.

Few people were on the avenue on this sunny but chilly day. Spring was definitely in the air though. A few birds had returned and buds were beginning to appear on the bare trees.

When they reached the playground, Bobby guided Sonny towards a bench near some men who were playing dominoes. A few other men stood around to coach and encourage the players. It was a lively game.

"Sonny, Bobby, how are you two boys doing on this fine day?" Mr. Williams greeted them. In his seventies, Mr. Williams was Mrs. Griffin's close friend. Bobby and Sonny had met him during their search for their neighbor. A short, lean, muscular man, with a dark complexion, Mr. Williams was quiet spoken and amiable. A dapper dresser, today Mr. Williams was wrapped up in his heavy winter coat despite the season change. A pipe hung from his mouth. He studied the pattern before selecting one of his bones. Then popped it down on the table blocking another man's move and winning the game.

"Gotcha," he laughed. "Do you want to play a round?" Mr. Williams asked Sonny.

"How can he play? He can't see." One of the old men grumbled.

"Bet he can beat you," Mr. Williams said. "Don't worry," he assured them. "I'm gonna coach him if he needs my help." Both Bobby and Mr. Williams knew Sonny's skill at dominoes. He'd beaten them many times. And sure enough, he won the game this time, too.

"Well, where are you boys off to?" Mr. Williams said as the boys prepared to leave.

"We gonna go hear the bongo players; then we gonna be hunting for wild animals," Bobby said.

"Watch out for bears and mountain lions," Mr. Williams said good-naturedly and waved them on their way before settling down for another game of dominoes with any takers.

"You know, I was thinking about what Mrs. Mobley said this morning," Sonny said as they walked.

"About what?"

"About something going on in the building."

"What's going on in the building?" Bobby asked, unusual for a boy who normally knew everything that went on in his neighborhood.

"I don't know. It's just a feeling," Sonny said. "It's like people are getting mad at each other a lot more often lately," recalling this morning's argument he heard between the Washingtons.

"No kidding, The Washingtons arguing?" Aside from Mrs. Griffin, Mr. and Mrs. Washington were the quietest, most generous people in the building. Bobby had never heard Mr. Washington raise his voice to his wife. He was always bringing her flowers and candy. Mr. Washington worked as a chef at one of the big hotels in midtown Manhattan, while Mrs. Washington was a stock clerk at Blumberg's, a department store on 125th Street. Sometimes he'd bring home leftover slices of turkey, ham and other goodies and share them with the residents of the building.

They kept walking until they reached the circle of drummers beating out steady rhythms on an assortment of instruments. A handful of bystanders swayed to the rhythms, cheering on the drummers each trying to outdo the other. The driving beats pushed one young woman into the center of the circle as she whirled to the music, her head bobbing up and down. Bobby and Sonny listened as one rhythm melted into another, seamless changes making it difficult to tell where one song ended and another began. After a while, Bobby whispered to Sonny, "Lets go over to the playground."

As they strolled down the path to the monkey bars and swings, they heard a little child crying.

"Stop all that crying," the child's mother scolded.

She stood beside a carriage holding the arm of a child about four years old. The child was rubbing her eyes and pointing to a patch of shrub in the distance.

"I can't be chasing after your ball every time you throw it somewhere."

"Don't worry," Bobby called to the mother. "I'll get it."

He steered Sonny to a nearby bench. "Be right back," he said and dashed off to retrieve the little girl's ball.

Sonny sat down to wait, aware that he was not alone on the bench. Taking up a goodly portion was a figure asleep. A man lay beneath a blanket of newspapers. His snores suddenly stopped, he sat up. As he shifted, Sonny was assailed by a strong odor of unwashed clothes. He leaned over to Sonny.

"Say kid. You got any money on you? I'm hungry."

Sonny felt his heartbeat quicken. "No sir," he said trying to keep his voice from trembling. Remembering his old fears when he was afraid even to leave his house, he gripped the edge of the bench and wished Bobby would hurry back. When Sonny was much younger and lived in another city with his mother, Charlotte had trusted a teenager in the neighborhood to look after her son while she went to work. The girl had taken him out for a walk. Preoccupied with her boyfriend, she forgot all about her charge. Some neighborhood boys decided to play a prank on him. They lured him into the middle of the street and he'd been hit by a car. Though not seriously injured, he was traumatized. Charlotte kept him inside the apartment, afraid to allow him outside for fear he'd be hurt again. If it had not been for Bobby, he'd probably still be there.

"What time is it? Ain't you supposed to be in school?" Not waiting for an answer, the man gathered up his papers and stuffed them into an already overstuffed shopping cart and moved away.

"Ready to go home?" Bobby sat down beside him.

"Do you see that man that just left?" Sonny asked. "What does he look like?"

Looking at the man who had gone a little distance from them, he said, "Him, he's just a bum." Bobby described as much as he could see of the man's retreating back.

"A bum? What do you mean?"

"A guy that live on the street."

"Why would anybody want to live on the street. Doesn't he have a home?"

Bobby shrugged. "I dunno. Guess not."

As they came to the corner store, Bobby suggested they go in and buy some candy. "My treat."

Sonny made a mental note to ask his mother why a person would rather live on the street than in a nice warm home.

Chapter Two

*A*fter Mrs. Thompson put the last dish on the table and sat down, Mr. Thompson bowed his head, "Let's say grace." Everyone bowed their heads except Bobby who kept one eye open as he surveyed the table, inhaling the aromas coming from his mother's fricassee chicken, mashed potatoes, and peas. He couldn't wait for his father to finish the prayer. Anticipating the ending he reached over for a piece of cornbread. "Bobby!" his mother scolded. He withdrew his hand and placed it in his lap.

"You act like you ain't ate in a week," Brenda said, folding her napkin ladylike and lifting her plate for Mrs. Thompson to fill. Bobby rolled his eyes at his sister trying to act grown.

"What did you do on your first day of vacation?" Mr. Thompson asked his children.

Bobby shrugged, "Nothing. Except Sonny and me went over to the park for a while."

"My girlfriends and I went to the movies," Brenda said suddenly remembering her recent elocution lesson with Mrs. Griffin's. "We saw…" She launched into a detailed critique of a musical she'd seen going on so long, Mrs. Thompson had to stop her.

"That's nice. Now eat your dinner before it gets cold."

"Joe," Mrs. Thompson turned to her husband. "Have you noticed anything strange going on around here?"

"Here? Have you children been doing something you shouldn't?" he asked looking at Bobby who shook his head.

"Not here." Mrs. Thompson corrected. "I mean in the building? Something's not like it should be."

Bobby's ears perked up, his interest momentarily distracted from the comic book he had hidden beneath the table.

"What do you mean?"

"Maybe it's my imagination," Mrs. Thompson shrugged. "But it seems…." A knock on the door interrupted.

"Who could that be and at dinner time?" Mr. Thompson said frowning.

Brenda jumped up, "I'll get it," She dashed down the hall to the door. "Make sure you ask who it is first." Mrs. Thompson warned.

Brenda came back shortly. "It's Mrs. Mobley. She wants to borrow a cup of sugar."

Mrs. Mobley stepped up behind Brenda. "Sorry to borrow you folks at dinnertime. I know I sure don't like to be bothered when I'm eating, but I need some sugar for the cake I'm baking for Mr. Mobley's birthday."

"No problem at all," Mrs. Thompson got up and signaled for Mrs. Mobley to follow her. Before she did, Mrs. Mobley stood looking over Bobby's shoulder at the food on the table. "My, my. That sure looks good."

"Would you like some?" Mr. Thompson asked, reaching for a small plate and holding it up to Mrs. Mobley who took it readily.

"Just a taste." She speared a chicken leg, the one Bobby had been eyeing, and placed it on her plate, taking a bite as she went into the kitchen.

After she left, Mrs. Thompson sat down again. Picking up the conversation from before, she said, "That's what I mean about something strange going on. Mrs. Mobley said she thought she had just bought a bag of sugar yesterday at the market, but when she went to look for it, it was gone."

"She probably thinks she bought a bag. But you know how she is," Mr. Thompson responded. "Forgetful."

"Well, I don't know. It seems like everybody in the building I've talked to lately has had an attack of forgetfulness. Mrs. Washington said her husband couldn't find his favorite shirt. The other day Miss Clark, you know the lady that lives on the fifth floor with her mother? She told me she'd bought a chicken from the market and swore she put it in the refrigerator. But when she went to look for it, it wasn't there."

"Is she the one that wears those tight dresses and high heels, the one with all the boyfriends?" Brenda chimed in. "Probably one of her boyfriends took it."

"Bren, how many times I've gotta tell you to stay out of grown folks' conversation," Mrs. Thompson admonished her.

"Yeah, she always butting into everybody's business," Bobby said.

"You, too," Mr. Thompson scolded. Brenda stuck her tongue out at her brother.

So, Sonny was right, Bobby thought. His mother, too, felt something was going on in the building, and for Mrs. Mobley to borrow sugar, this was a first. Something definitely was going on.

Downstairs in Apartment 2C Sonny and his mother Charlotte had finished dinner. Seated on the couch, with his head in her lap, Sonny listened intently as his mother read another chapter of *Treasure Island* to him.

"Mom, why do people live in the street?" he asked suddenly.

"Where did that come from?" She put the book down on the coffee table and gently moving him aside, she rose and went into the kitchen. "Who told you people live in the street?" He heard the refrigerator open and shut. Charlotte returned carrying a tray on which sat two glasses of milk and two pieces of cake she'd picked up at the market.

"Bobby and I saw a bum in the park. He was sleeping on a bench."

"You shouldn't call a person a bum just because they don't have a place to stay. Sometimes people lose their homes because they can't pay their rent. There's all sorts of reasons a person is homeless. If I was to lose my job and couldn't pay the rent, we'd be out on the street, too." Their plates empty, Sonny took them into the kitchen and rinsed them out. When he returned, he asked his mother, "Can we play dominoes later?"

Charlotte yawned. "Let me finish this chapter, then one game and off to bed with you."

Chapter Three

The next afternoon, all was quiet in the building. Bobby had gone with Brenda to visit their Aunt Mandy who lived on 116th Street. Mrs. Mobley had gone to the market. Mrs. Vincent was in bed with the flu. Mr. Brown, the super, was in his basement apartment sleeping off last night's hangover. The building had been swept, the trashcans removed and placed in the backyard until trash day. He'd done all his pressing chores. Now was his time.

Alone in his bedroom, Sonny sat reading the latest book Charlotte had bought him, a book about Africa. He loved books about far away places. One day, he hoped to visit Ethiopia or maybe Egypt. At one point he felt a sudden breeze as if the door had opened. "Mama?" he called wondering if Charlotte had come home early. No one answered. He listened, then shrugged. He must have made a mistake. Feeling hungry, he thought about having another piece of the cake Charlotte had bought and a glass of milk. Walking into the kitchen, he stopped and sniffed. A spasm of fear surged through his body. That smell, the same smell of unwashed clothes as in the park, seemed to hang in the air. Someone was nearby. Sonny felt his presence. Backing away, he quickly retreated to his room, locking the door behind him and pushing a chair up against it. He rushed to his closet and burying himself beneath a mountain of clothes, he waited for his mother.

*   *   *   *

"Well, I'll be! Bobby, did you take a bath and forget to wash out the tub? You know better than that," Mrs. Thompson chided when she got home that evening.

"No, Mama. I ain't been near the bathtub today. Must be Brenda."

Mrs. Thompson called to Brenda who entered the bathroom to see her mother standing over the tub with her hands on her hips. Bobby stood just behind them. Around the inside of the tub was a thick dark ring. On the floor were several damp towels.

"Who made this mess?"

Bobby and Brenda looked at each other, then at their mother. "Maybe Daddy did," they said at the same time.

"How could your father have done this? He's been at work all day," Mrs. Thompson responded. "I'll ask him when he comes in tonight." She sighed her anger abating somewhat. As she picked up the damp towels, she said, "Bobby, you and Brenda gather the dirty clothes together and take them downstairs to the laundry. I'll clean up in here before your father gets home."

"If it wasn't Daddy who made the ring, and it wasn't you or me, who done it?" Bobby wondered as he and Brenda hauled two bundles of laundry down the stairs to the laundry room.

"You always trying to make something out of nothing. You probably did it and don't remember." After loading up the washing machine, she said, "I'll be right back. I promised Beverly, I'd return her magazine. You watch the clothes."

"You better hurry back or I'll tell."

"What's wrong? You scared to be down here by yourself?" Brenda teased as she ran out the door.

It wasn't that Bobby was afraid to be in the laundry room by himself. He just felt uneasy. Beyond the room, the basement was filled with shadows. Long pipes hung along the low ceiling made the overhead light bulb seem even dimmer. Along the wall stood huge storage cases filled with old furniture, mattresses and other discards Mr. Brown hadn't thrown away yet. At the far end the coal bin sat beneath a small window.

The walls of the bin were coated with soot. Back in the far corner was where Mr. Brown lived, his tiny apartment door barely noticeable.

Bobby had brought two comic books with him. Trying to concentrate on the stories was hard. Above his head, he could hear the sounds of footsteps. Through the pipes he heard voices, snatches of conversations. Despite the comfort in knowing he wasn't really alone, he didn't like being in the basement. He wished he'd asked Sonny to come with him. He hadn't spoken to his friend all day, he remembered. He'd knock on his way back upstairs when he finished doing the laundry.

So absorbed in Dick Tracy, he didn't hear the door to the laundry room open. Vaguely aware, he heard the sound of water running into a tub. Thinking it was one of the tenants, he kept reading. A loud persistent cough made him look up. At the far end of the room, Bobby saw the figure of a huge man, bent over one of the washing machines. He wore a sweater and dark pants. He began to pull the sweater over his head.

"Mr. Washington," Bobby called. "I'm glad to see you. I don't like being down here by myself." Suddenly, Bobby froze. It wasn't Mr. Washington!

At the sound of Bobby's voice, the man stopped, his hands in mid air, the sweater covering his face and neck. With his back to Bobby, he pulled his sweater down around him, grabbed his bundle and rushed quickly to the door before Bobby could see his face.

"It was weird," Bobby reported to Brenda when she returned. "He just ran out without even closing the lid on the machine." Bobby went over and peered into the washing machine. Inside were several items of clothes, one of which was a blue shirt.

"Maybe he went to get washing powder, stupid. You think everything is weird," Brenda responded as she and Bobby folded up the last of the towels.

"It been over an hour and he ain't come back yet."

"Maybe he had to go to the store to buy stuff. Come on. Let's get back upstairs." Brenda shook her head. "You and your wild imagination. Always making something out of nothing."

As they approached Apartment 2C, Bobby said, "You go on up. I'm gonna stop by Sonny's for a minute."

"And how I'm gonna get the laundry upstairs by myself?"

Bobby grabbed his bundle and taking two steps at a time, deposited his load at his door. Passing Brenda on his way back down to Apartment 2C, he stuck out his tongue at her.

At Sonny's door, he knocked. Charlotte answered, a worried look on her face.

"Can I talk to Sonny for a minute?"

"He's in his room. He had a bad fright today. Sonny says somebody broke into the apartment today. I called the police but they didn't find anything missing. They think it was his imagination. I don't know about that." Bobby followed Charlotte down the hall to Sonny's room.

"Bobby's here to see you. Can I get you something to drink? I'd offer you a piece of cake but Sonny must have eaten it all up. For one so skinny, he loves his sweets almost as much as I do," she smiled.

Sonny was lying in bed, his head turned toward the wall. After his mother left, he sat up. He hurried to tell Bobby about the incident earlier.

"The police came today. They said it was my imagination, but I know somebody came in. I heard him."

Bobby assured Sonny that he believed him. Then he told Sonny about the strange incidents that happened at his place, the dirty tub, and about the man he saw in the basement.

"We got some investigating to do. I think somebody be hiding out in the building, a robber, or an escaped convict."

Sonny appeared frightened. "Are you sure we've got to do it? Can't we tell a grown up, like Mr. Brown or you dad?"

"They ain't gonna believe us. We got to do it ourselves. When we got proof, then we'll tell them."

As Bobby was about to leave, Sonny called, "I didn't eat any cake today."

"Huh?" Bobby said, "what cake?"

"I said, I didn't eat the cake. The cake Mama bought yesterday. I did-n't eat it."

"So?" Bobby didn't understand what cake had to do with their discussion.

"The man who came in must have eaten it."

"You mean, the reason the police didn't find nothin missing is because the only thing the man took was cake?"

"Yes," Sonny said, feeling suddenly relieved. "Then he wasn't after me. He was hungry."

They heard the doorbell ring and Brenda's voice. "Mama says for Bobby to come home."

"Tomorrow we got a lot of work to do," Bobby said as he headed for the door.

"Right, sir." Sonny saluted him. "First thing." Only, he wasn't so sure.

Chapter Four

*I*t was Thursday and with only two days of their spring vacation left, Bobby and Sonny met early, right after their folks left for work. Brenda left early, too, to spend the day with her friends on the next block. The building was quiet. Not even Mrs. Mobley or Mrs. Vincent, the building sentinels, were on their post.

"Where should we start?" Sonny asked.

"We betta start in the basement. We could ask Mr. Brown if he seen anything strange."

"Good idea. But what are we gonna do if we find the person?"

Bobby scratched his head. "I ain't thought about that. I guess we be knowing when we find him."

The boys headed down the basement steps to Mr. Brown's apartment. Despite the sunny day, in the basement the only light came in from the window near the coal chute. Bobby guided Sonny around the stacked boxes, past the laundry room which was dark, and over to Mr. Brown's door. He knocked. The sound on the metal door reverberated throughout the basement. The boys stood back and waited. Knowing Mr. Brown didn't care much for people, especially young people, the boys felt nervous. They waited for almost five minutes but no answer.

"Maybe he's in the backyard," Sonny said. "Should we try to find him before we go searching?"

Always ready for an adventure, Bobby responded. "Naw, if we find anything, we can let him know."

They began their search in the basement, Bobby describing what he saw to Sonny who sat on a mattress in the corner of the large room. Next he checked the storage room climbing behind more boxes, old furniture, lamps, dressers and a discarded bicycle left by some tenant long gone.

"Hey," Bobby shouted. "Come over here and see this great bike somebody left."

Following his friend's voice, Sonny made his way to the storage room door. Seated astride a man's bicycle, Bobby pretended he was racing around the neighborhood. He got off and guided Sonny over to it, describing its appearance to Sonny who ran his hands over the frame.

"It's rusty and be needing a lot of work," Bobby said. "I wonder who it belong to. If I had a bike like this…"

"What are you kids doing down here?" Mr. Brown stood in the doorway. "You got no business down here in the storage room!" He lumbered over to Bobby and took the bike from him. "I'm gonna tell your parents, and you're gonna get a whipping. Now get going."

"But Mr. Brown, we came looking for you." Bobby tried to explain.

"That's why you down here playing with this old bike, I suppose," he said sarcastically.

"We came to ask you if you noticed anything unusual going on in the building," Sonny said.

Mr. Brown laughed. "I don't have time to notice nothing except how you kids always tearing things up here. Now if you excuse me, I got work to do. He locked the storage room door and ushered the boys to the door. "If I catch you boys anywhere you ain't suppose to be…." His voice trailed off as the boys hastened up the stairs to the street.

"Now what are we gonna do?" Sonny asked.

"Let's go up to the roof and work our way down."

"But you heard what Mr. Brown said. He's gonna tell our parents we were snooping in the basement."

"He always making threats. And what if he do. We not breaking no laws," Bobby shrugged. "Let's get started before somebody else be coming."

Sonny followed Bobby up the six flights of stairs to the roof. He'd never been above the third floor, Bobby's apartment, and as they climbed, he felt his stomach muscles tighten.

When they reached the door to the roof, Bobby tried the handle, but though the handle turned, the door didn't budge.

"Somethin's blocking the door. Help me push it open." The boys put their shoulders against the door and pushed. Slowly, the door opened with a loud creak. Bright sunlight and a stiff breeze greeted them. In the distance, Bobby could see the roofs of apartment buildings spread out in all directions. He could even see the skyscrapers of downtown Manhattan as they towered above the shorter buildings. Bobby walked over to the edge and peered down at the street. A sudden fear gripped his stomach as it did whenever he looked down from a great height. Below except for a few people walking to and fro, little activity marked the mid morning streets. He could see Colonial Park in the distance with its trees, patches of grass, and the empty public swimming pool. In a couple of months, it would be open for the summer onslaught.

"See anything unusual?" Sonny's voice called him back. Sonny stood in the doorway, his hands gripping the doorframe.

Bobby described the landscape. "It's awesome, but I ain't suppose to be up here. My dad told me that some years ago, when I was a little kid, the police caught this guy up on this roof. They say he robbed and killed some old woman who lived in the next block. And the guy use to live in this building." He shivered.

"If you didn't find anything, can we go down now. I don't like it up here."

"You right. There ain't no place for nobody to be hiding." Bobby said taking one last look. Way over to the side, Bobby spotted a stack of crates, behind which was a small structure. No door was visible on the outside. Dismissing it as too narrow for anyone to live in, he joined Sonny and together they descended the stairs.

Bobby shook his head in disappointment. "I was so sure we'd find somebody living here that don't belong. One thing's for sure, somebody's breaking into everybody's apartments. Who you think it is?"

"Maybe it's not an intruder. Maybe it's somebody who lives here," Sonny said.

"No way. I know practically everybody in the building. It's got to be a whatchu call it? a intruder, whatever that means. Besides, if it was somebody living here, why would he be taking a bath in our bathtub? And why would he be sneaking in your apartment just to eat cake? It gotta be somebody from outside."

"You're probably right," Sonny said. "So maybe our next move should be to find out all the things that are missing."

"Which means," Bobby added, "We gotta question everybody in the building."

"School will be starting on Monday. After that we won't have any time."

"Then we better start as soon as possible. Most people be home on Saturday. We could ask them on Saturday."

"Do you think they'll listen to us?" Sonny asked.

"We just gotta take our chances."

Chapter Five

When the boys told Mrs. Griffin about their plan, she was skeptical at first. Though she was missing a small change bank with a collection of coins from various parts of the world, coins that her late husband had given her, she thought she'd mislaid it. Now she wasn't so sure.

"How can I help?" She asked the boys.

"We gotta talk to everybody and ask if they seen anything," Bobby said.

"Saw anything," Mrs. Griffin corrected.

"We thought about knocking on everybody's door and asking them. But that would take some time," said Sonny.

"Why don't I invite the tenants here to my place for a meeting?" Mrs. Griffin suggested. "Then you can question them all together."

"That's a great idea!" Bobby responded.

Sonny thought so too. He added, "Do you think they'll come?"

"It's worth a try. I'll throw a party. Long ago, before you two were born, I use to have parties all the time. All the neighbors would come especially when they knew a celebrated guest just might drop in. My husband knew many entertainers. Once the great Fats Waller stopped by and played on that very piano." Mrs. Griffin went on dreamily. Standing by her upright, Sonny's hands gently caressed the polished ivory. He'd played on the same piano used by Fats Waller. He could hardly wait to tell his mother.

Bobby's mind, however, was on the gathering Mrs. Griffin would organize. How would he get everybody to cooperate? Would they believe the boys' theory about an intruder?

"Could we have it on Saturday?" he asked.

"Two days from now? I don't know. There's so much work to do. First we'll have to send out invitations. Next I'll have to get together a menu and shop for food." Mrs. Griffin's voice sparkled with excitement.

"What you want us to do?" Sonny asked.

The next day, Friday, Mrs. Griffin handed the boys a stack of invitations to be distributed throughout the building. They went from door to door knocking and when they got no answer, they slipped the invitations beneath the door. Soon the building was abuzz with conversations about Mrs. Griffin's party which was set for the next evening.

*   *   *   *

"Why is Mrs. Griffin throwing a party and inviting all the grownups in the building?" Brenda asked her mother as Mr. and Mrs. Thompson prepared to go downstairs.

"I don't know. She use to give parties all the time. But that was a long time ago even before we moved here. They say she and Mr. Griffin were known for their parties. I don't think there's anybody in the building except maybe Mrs. Vincent who has been here as long as Mrs. Griffin. We'll just have to go and see. By the way, when Bobby gets home, be sure to tell him to take out the garbage and to clean up his room," Mrs. Thompson said.

"Where is Bobby?" Mr. Thompson asked.

"He's probably down at Sonny's. It's hard to keep up with him these days."

They could hear the music coming from behind Mrs. Griffin's door before they reached the bottom step. Duke Ellington's "Stomping at the Savoy" greeted the newcomers. The room was already filled with neighbors from the apartments throughout the building. Mr. and Mrs. Thompson said hello to several they knew and others they knew only by sight as they passed each other on the staircase occasionally. Mr. Thompson drifted over to Mr. Washington who stood against the wall and was soon engaged in conversation. Feeling awkward, Mrs.

Thompson, who didn't socialize much, sought out Mrs. Griffin and asked her if she needed any help.

"No, thank you, my dear. I've got my two little helpers in the kitchen along with Mrs. Henderson."

Though the invitation said to dress informally as most of the guests were, Mrs. Griffin was dressed in a long blue lace gown, her favorite, a fashion from the twenties. Her fine gray hair was pinned into an upsweep that made her look years younger than a woman in her seventies. She smiled and greeted all the guests graciously, welcoming them to her home and enlightening them with a little history not only of the neighborhood, but also of the culture, knowledge she readily shared with Sonny, Bobby, and the neighborhood children.

The kitchen door swung open and Bobby entered carrying a tray of hors d'oeuvres. He went around the room serving everyone until his tray was empty. Mrs. Thompson frowned in surprise when she saw her son.

"I thought you were at Sonny's. What are you doing here?"

Drawing her aside, Bobby told her of his and Sonny's plan. His mother shook her head and sighed. "I should have known. And where's Sonny? In the kitchen I suppose."

Everyone seemed to be enjoying themselves. On the loveseat sat Mrs. Mobley and Mrs. Vincent surveying the room. As Bobby walked past, he heard them commenting on Mrs. Griffin's decor. Mrs. Washington was seated between the Emerson sisters, twins that lived on the fifth floor. They talked over her. She seemed uncomfortable with her hands folded in her lap as she watched her husband and Mr. Thompson. The doorbell rang and in walked Miss Clark. A slender woman in her thirties with short, curly hair, she wore a bright red tight fitting low cut dress and high heel platform shoes, as if she were on her way to a party, not this one.

"Sorry I'm late and I can't stay long. So what's up?"

Mrs. Griffin asked, "I'm glad you came. How's your mother?"

"Mom's fine." She glanced around the room and seeing Joe Thompson and Marvin Washington standing together, she switched over to them.

"How ya doing, fellows?"

Taking out a cigarette, she waited for either of them to light it for her. Of course, all eyes were on her.

"Humpf!" Mrs. Vincent said, disapprovingly.

Mrs. Mobley shook her head and averted her eyes, "Some people!" she muttered.

Mrs. Griffin approached her and whispered in her ear. Putting the unlit cigarette back into the pack, Miss Clark strolled over to the windowsill, sat down, and picking up a Jet magazine, began leafing through it.

The doorbell rang again and in walked Mr. Brown.

"So glad you could make it. Now that you're here, we can get started." Mrs. Griffin turned off the phonograph. Eyeing the group suspiciously, Mr. Brown and moved over to lean against an empty corner of the wall.

Bobby, Sonny, and Charlotte emerged from the kitchen.

"I hope you all are enjoying yourselves," said Mrs. Griffin. "We should do this more often. It's important that we know our neighbors, don't you think? Now first, I'll tell you why we asked you all here, this evening. Then I'll turn the meeting over to Bobby and Sonny whom you all know. Afterwards, we'll settle down and have the fine meal I wouldn't have been able to prepare without the help of Charlotte Henderson and her two helpers Sonny and Bobby." She made sure she had everyone's attention before going on.

"I asked you all here tonight to discuss the recent rash of missing things and unusual happenings that are going on in the building."

Sonny felt the silence. Just as suddenly he heard a murmur of voices that seemed to rise in pitch. His mother's arms around his shoulders comforted him, but not much.

"Please give these boys your attention and cooperation."

Bobby stood just behind Sonny and Charlotte. Butterflies fluttered in his stomach, and when Charlotte moved aside to let him stand beside Sonny, his knees began to knock. He opened his mouth to speak but only a hoarse croak came out. He nudged Sonny.

"The other day when I was home by myself, I heard the door open." Sonny began, his voice trembling and low. "Speak louder," Charlotte urged.

"At first I thought it was my mother, then I knew it wasn't and I got scared. Somebody took the rest of the cake Mama had brought home,"

Laughter broke out in the room. "He probably ate it and forgot."

"Maybe a mouse ate it."

"So what's this got to do with us?" Miss Clark asked, glancing down at her watch.

"We think somebody be hiding out in the building?" Bobby found his voice. Again everyone started talking at once.

"I'm hungry. Where's the food?" Mr. Washington said, smiling over at his wife.

"Do anybody got anything missing?" Bobby went on.

"If somebody's hiding in the building, Mr. Brown would know."

They turned to the super who shook his head and started for the door.

"Ain't nobody hiding out in this building. Just these crazy kids' imagination. I ain't got time for this." He opened the door.

"Wait just a minute. You got to hear these boys out. You can't dismiss what they have to say so quickly," Mr. Thompson leaped to their defense. "Now, I know these youngsters like to make up stories, I did too, when I was their age, but I think we should hear them out."

"My boy don't lie!" Charlotte put in, moving in front of the boys. "It may seem like a little thing, a piece of cake missing. I thought he probably ate it too, at first. Now I'm not so sure. You all need to listen to what they got to say. Go head boys."

Bobby told about overhearing Mrs. Mobley's conversation with Mrs. Vincent about how she felt something strange was going on in the building.

"I said I felt something wasn't right…Anyway, you shouldn't be listening to other people's conversation." Mrs. Mobley nodded to Mrs. Vincent who gripped her pocketbook closer to her chest.

"What about Mr. Washington's favorite shirt?" Sonny asked, his voice stronger.

"And the missing chicken?" Bobby added.

"And the dirty bathtub?" Mrs. Thompson said hesitantly. All eyes turned to her. "Yes, the dirty bathtub." She related the bathtub incident. "I thought at the time that Bobby had done it. Now, like Mrs. Henderson said, I'm not so sure either."

By now, the neighbors were comparing notes. This was missing, that was missing, little things that would normally go unnoticed. Small change, food items, a blanket, socks, a razor.

"Hold on," Mr. Brown spoke defensively. "Yall not accusing me, are you? Cause if you are…"

"We're not accusing you," Mrs. Griffin hastened to calm the gathering.

"There may be some truth to what these boys are saying. Someone may hiding out in the building and entering our apartments when no one's at home."

"Kinda scary," one of the Emerson twins remarked.

"So Mr. Brown, what are you gonna do about it?" Mrs. Vincent demanded.

"What am I gonna do about it? It's you all's problem. I ain't missing nothing. My job is to keep the place clean, put out the garbage and see that you get enough heat in the winter. I ain't the police."

"What about the police?" someone asked. "Shouldn't we call them?"

"You think they'd investigate a missing piece of cake or a chicken leg? Or even a shirt? They'd laugh in our faces."

"So what can we do?"

Throughout the exchange, Bobby and Sonny had been forgotten. Bobby stepped forward. "I think I seen the man when I was downstairs in the laundry room."

"And you didn't tell us?" Bobby's mother asked with alarm.

"You could've been hurt," Mr. Thompson said.

"I think it was him. He had on Mr. Washington's blue shirt. I thought it was Mr. Washington. When I called him, he ran away."

"In my favorite shirt?" Mr. Washington shook his head.

"Wonder what he was doing in the laundry room?" Mrs. Washington asked.

"Probably trying to steal the machine. Good thing Bobby was there." Mrs. Vincent remarked.

"Probably doing his laundry."

"Yeah, washing the things he stole."

"At least he's a clean burglar. He can't be all bad," Miss Clark said.

"Regardless of whether he's a clean burglar or not, he's still committing a crime."

"Yes, and what are we gonna do about it?"

"Sonny and me got a plan." Bobby said. Sonny swallowed hard. This was the first he'd heard of it. Everybody's eyes were on the pair.

"We can't tell you now. But soon. We gonna catch the intruder, don't worry. For now, everybody betta lock they doors and windows," he advised.

The delicious aromas from the dining room seeped into the room capturing the attention of the gathering. One by one they drifted over to the table until Bobby and Sonny found themselves alone in the living room.

"Plan, what plan?" Sonny asked.

"I don't know. Tomorrow we gotta think up one. Right now, I'm hungry."

They dashed over to the line formed around the buffet table.

Chapter Six

*T*he meeting over, all the neighbors returned to their respective apartments.

"So, what do you think?" Mrs. Vincent's voice echoed against the walls of the darkened hallway as she and Mrs. Mobley climbed the stairs to their apartment. "Do you think there really is somebody living here that we don't know about?" She stopped in front of her door.

"Like I told you before. Something's going on. I don't know if them children know what they're talking about, but whatever it is, I'm gonna be on the look out." Mrs. Mobley looked up at the next flight of stairs and stood with her hand on the newel post. Waiting until her breath slowed, she opened her purse, took out her handkerchief and mopped her brow. "Sure wish they'd put an elevator in this building and more lights."

"That'd be the day. You want to come in for a spell?"

"Naw, just trying to catch my breath. Theodore should be home from work. I'll see you in the morning."

Mrs. Vincent watched as Mrs. Mobley made her way with effort up the stairs to the fourth floor. Then she closed her door.

The lights were out in the corridor which wasn't unusual. Mrs. Mobley's steps quickened as she neared her door. As she pressed her key into the lock, it opened with little effort. Startled, at first, until she remembered Theodore, her husband. "He probably heard me coming and left the door unlocked." She sighed with relief as she entered the dimly lit apartment. Her husband lay on the sofa, the light from the TV illuminating the outline of his bulky frame.

"Teddy, you shoulda been down at Mrs. Griffin's tonight." She spoke in a loud voice. "All the neighbors was there. Mrs. Griffin got a nice place though too cluttered for my taste. I think it looks like a museum…" her voice trailed off as she moved to the bedroom. A figure stood in the shadows, hidden behind the heavy curtains that flanked the windows. He held his breath as he watched the woman kick off her shoes and struggle to unzip her dress before walking to the bedroom. On the sofa, her husband's loud snore suddenly stopped midway, waking him momentarily. He turned over and resumed his sleep. The way clear, the figure crouched down and began to make his way towards the door.

"Teddy, wake up! Turn that TV off and come to bed." Mrs. Mobley, now dressed in her nightgown outlined the bedroom door. Her hands on her hips, she peered into the living room.

"What? Huh?" Mr. Mobley shifted and sat up.

"Come to bed. I told you not to fall asleep on the couch. You know how it messes up your back."

"Yeah," he muttered getting up and lumbering pass his wife; he headed for the bathroom.

"Did you cut the TV off and check to see that the door is locked?" she called.

The man, reaching the door, quietly opened it and slipped out.

Shaking her head in annoyance, she strode into the living room, turned off the TV and then over to the door and secured the police bolt.

*   *   *   *

Larry Clayton bolted up the stairs to the roof as fast as he could taking two steps at a time. In his bag he carried the remains of the Mobley's dinner, a few pieces of ham, several slices of bread, and a bottle of beer, along with a slice of apple pie. He rushed to the far corner of the roof, shoved aside the crates he'd place there to obscure the entrance to the storage bin, opened the door and went inside.

It was a tiny room but made cozy with the things he'd acquired since taking up residence there a few weeks ago. A single cot stood against the wall surrounded by boxes of various sizes containing forgotten things left by former tenants. He'd gone through some of them and had found useful items. Some he'd stuffed in his duffel bag, others like a crudely made quilt and windup clock he set out to keep track of the time. Beside the clock he'd placed a picture of his daughter, Denise. She must be at least five years old now. His mother had sent him the photograph when he was in Korea.

On one wall hung some movie posters he'd gotten from the Odeon Theatre when they'd changed the feature film. One poster advertised "From Here to Eternity," with Burt Lancaster and Deborah Kerr huddled in an embrace on the beach as the waves crashed over them. Another advertising "Battle Ground" hung on the other.

Larry finished off his meal and lay down. His head pounding, he drifted off to sleep. He sat up suddenly. "Gotta get to the hill, gotta get the supplies to the men."

Shifting the boxes from one side of the room to the other, he yelled, "Hey Doc, where's the keys? How am I gonna get the supplies to the men if I can't find the keys to the truck." He searched his pockets. "Yall playing with me?" He whirled around. "Why you hiding from me?" Suddenly he dropped down to his knees and covered his head as the bombs dropped all around him. His heart beat rapidly, sweat poured down his face. "No, watch out! Watch out!" he screamed trying to curl himself up into a ball for protection. "You not gonna get me." Then, just as suddenly, all was quiet. Slowly, he opened his eyes.

Looking around the tiny room, he remembered where he was. His clothes drenched, he reached for a towel and wiped his face. He peeled off the shirt he'd taken from Mr. Washington's closet and spread it out to dry on top of an old forgotten suitcase that belonged to a tenant long since moved. Putting on a flannel robe he'd taken from another neighbor, he sat down to enjoy the apple of pie. When he had finished it and had put the room back in order, he stepped out onto the rooftop. The evening was clear and mild. A few stars dotted the sky, and in the distance he could just make out the lights from downtown and the Empire State Building. Below, the neighborhood streets were quiet, an occasional cab whizzed by. Few people walked the streets. He finished his cigarette and lit another, reluctant to return to the little room he called home, dreading the nightmares that would surely come as soon as his head hit the pillow.

Chapter Seven

I got the list," Bobby said, pushing past Sonny and plopping down on his living room floor. "I went to all the neighbors' apartments this morning and they gave me a list of stuff that was missing. Mrs. Griffin's party did the trick. They wouldn't 've did it otherwise."

"You're right. Did they give you any dates when they discovered things were missing?" Sonny eased down beside him.

"Dates? What for?" Bobby scratched his head.

"Cause if we know the dates, then we can know how long the intruder's been coming in. Mr. Washington lost his shirt around the beginning of the week."

"How come you know that?"

"Cause that's when I heard them arguing. You remember. I told you I heard Mr. Washington and his wife arguing when he couldn't find his favorite shirt?"

"Yeah. But Mrs. Johnson said she ain't been able to find a set of new towels she bought early this month. And that's when it seem like everybody be getting mad at each other." Bobby shuffled through his notebook. "Hummm, let's see what I got. Mrs. Mobley couldn't find a bag of sugar she bought. She didn't say when. Miss Clark said somebody stole a chicken she baked for dinner."

"And don't forget the piece of cake from my house."

"Somebody's hungry."

"Don't forget whoever it was took a bath in your bathroom."

"Yeah, and washed his clothes in the laundry downstairs. Could it be somebody visiting?"

"What do you mean?" asked Sonny shifting his position on the floor.

"Mr. Brown's nephew was here."

"But wasn't that back in February? Things didn't start missing until this month."

"You're right." Bobby got up and began to pace the room. "What about one of Miss Clark's boyfriends? She always got visitors."

"Why would her boyfriends break into the neighbors' apartments to steal food? And besides, somebody came into her apartment too. No, I think somebody's living here that we don't know about.

"But we searched the building from top to bottom and nothing."

"Maybe we missed something."

"I've got it. Why don't we set a trap?" suggested Bobby. "We can use your apartment and…"

"Why my place?" The very thought sent shivers through Sonny. "Why not yours?"

"My parents wouldn't be going for that. Besides, the intruder already been inside my apartment. I don't think he be coming again."

"He's been here, too, and I hope he won't ever come back."

"Somebody's gotta be willing to help us set a trap." Bobby shook his head and continued to pace the room. Sonny rose and went into the kitchen to get a snack. It was going to be a long afternoon.

*   *   *   *

"I don't see any reason why you gotta use my apartment," Mrs. Vincent argued. "Just 'cause nothing's been missing is no reason I should invite trouble." She folded her arms over her flat chest and shook her head.

"Now Justine, the boys got a good plan. That's the only way we can catch this intruder. All you gotta do is let everybody know you gonna be out and they'll be hiding in your apartment to catch him." Mrs. Mobley spoke in her most persuasive voice to the woman sitting beside her. Bobby and Sonny sat on the steps in front of them not saying anything that would jeopardize their plan.

"Hump! these boys? And what are they gonna do? They ain't big enough to stop a mouse." Mrs. Vincent eyed the boys skeptically. "How they gonna stop a criminal?"

"Mr. Mobley has agreed to help out. He's gonna be right there with them," said Mrs. Mobley.

Bobby and Sonny had first approached Mrs. Mobley when they saw her sitting alone that afternoon. When they first told her their plan, she, too, was reluctant. But having remembered the argument she'd had with her husband early in the morning about the missing food and dishes, she agreed. Something must be done. Calling the police for what to them would seem trivial would be pointless. They'd simply patronize her as she'd seen them do to others with more serious crimes committed against them. At least the boys had a plan and it just might work. They told her they needed someone's apartment to use as bait. Going down their list of possible places, she suggested her friend Mrs. Vincent. "As far as I know, nobody's been to her place yet. I'm not sure she believes there is an intruder."

It took quite a bit of persuasion before Mrs. Vincent agreed to let the boys use her place. The plan was set for the following Saturday, Mr. Mobley's day off. Neither Bobby nor Sonny told their parents about the scheme not wanting them to worry. With Bobby and Sonny, seated around her breakfast table, Mrs. Vincent gave them last minute instructions. There was no need to go into the other rooms or touch any of her things. She expected everything to be in its rightful place when she returned in a few hours. They would find sandwiches and drink in the refrigerator. Mrs. Mobley had telephoned to say Mr. Mobley would be down as soon as he woke up.

Mrs. Vincent called out loudly as she stood in front of her apartment, "Alma, come on or we'll be late for the stores." Her voice reverberated throughout the hallway as was the plan.

"In a minute," Mrs. Mobley answered from her fourth floor landing. "Do you have the directions? It'll probably take us all day to get there and back."

"Newark's not that far. But you know how slow the busses are."

The women talked in voices loud enough to wake the entire building as they made their way to the street. Bobby watched them through Mrs. Vincent's living room window.

"They gone. Let's watch cartoons on TV."

"We can't turn on the television. The intruder will hear it and know somebody's here."

"I forgot. So what do we do while we wait?" Bobby wished now that he'd brought some of his comic books with him.

"I bought my dominoes." Sonny pulled out his box of dominoes and began setting them up on the kitchen table. Bobby wandered into the living room, peering around at the collection of photographs of Mrs. Vincent's relatives, he guessed. There was one picture of a young Mrs. Vincent in her wedding dress and a man Bobby assumed was the late Mr. Vincent, a handsome man in a sailor's uniform smiling into the camera and holding tightly to the woman beside him. Another black and white photograph of a naked baby lying on her stomach on a rug, and still another of a large family, several adults and children taken on a farm in front of a huge old white shingled house. "Must be her family," Bobby muttered to himself. It was faded as were the others. There was a photograph in color of a young couple on the beach. In the background, Bobby could see the sun's reflection bouncing off the waves. Mrs. Vincent's apartment was laid out like all the other apartments in the building. Still each had its own style. Mrs. Griffins was by far the most interesting to Bobby. Everything she had was connected to some fascinating story she'd told the boys.

Sonny heard the knock on the door first. It was barely audible.

"Somebody's at the door," Sonny said, his stomach doing flip-flops. "Do you think it's the intruder?"

"I don't think he would knock. Do you? Who is it?" whispered Bobby pressing his ear against the door.

"Open up, boys. It's me, Mobley."

Relief spread over the boys face as Bobby unlatched the door and moved aside to let Mr. Mobley in. A stout man with an equally rotund stomach, Mr. Mobley was around 5'7, a few inches taller than his wife.

His gray hair, the little remaining, was curly and fine and formed a circle around his shiny dome. His face was that of a man who laughed a lot. The boys liked him though they seldom saw him as he worked nights. Mr. Mobley was always quick to smile and quick to tell a joke. It was difficult to understand how he and Mrs. Mobley, who seemed the exact opposite, could have found something in common to allow them to have been married for over thirty years.

"So what are we supposed to be doing? My wife didn't tell me much except I'm to sit here with you two boys and wait for somebody to break in, right?"

After Sonny explained the situation and Bobby filled in the details, they decided they were hungry. Once they had finished eating and had cleaned up their dishes, Mr. Mobley challenged Sonny to a game of dominoes. Sonny won all the games. Meanwhile, Bobby watched cartoons with the sound muted. As the hours passed, Mr. Mobley stretched out on Mrs. Vincent's sofa and promptly fell asleep.

Mid afternoon, the boys began to wonder if the intruder would come after all. When Mrs. Vincent returned at 4 p.m. she found all three of them asleep.

"Seems like your plan didn't work," she told the boys after waking them and after checking to see that everything was in order. "Couldn't even enjoy myself thinking about what was going on in my absence."

"If somebody had come in, they could have tiptoed over your sleeping bodies and taken everything in the place," Mrs. Mobley said.

"I'm a light sleeper. And I would have woke up if somebody had even tried to come in," said Bobby defensively.

"We're sorry we fell asleep," Sonny apologized.

Mr. Mobley stretched and yawned. "Mrs. Vincent, you got anything sweet, pie, cake?"

"Com'on, Teddy." Mrs. Mobley pulled her husband towards the door. "I'll fix dinner and dessert as soon as we get upstairs. Then you can go back to sleep."

"Sorry, we done put you through all that trouble," Bobby said as he and Sonny followed the Mobleys out.

"I still don't think there is an intruder," Mrs. Vincent said before closing the door. "All this trouble for nothing."

"Well, what are we going to do now?" Sonny asked.

"I dunno," Bobby shrugged.

Chapter Eight

Sunday afternoon was uneventful. Upstairs in his apartment, Bobby lay on the couch reading the latest issue of Dick Tracy while Brenda talked on the telephone. Their parents had gone out to visit friends. School would resume tomorrow. Sunday was a time to wind down and get ready for their early morning routine. After spending most of the morning in church, Charlotte prepared dinner then, after they'd eaten, went to her room to listen to "The Shadow," her favorite radio show. Sonny sat in his bedroom, sorting through his record collection before deciding what to listen to.

Suddenly, Sonny heard a click, the sound of a door opening. Fear raced down his spine. The intruder had entered their apartment! Sonny was sure of it. He wanted to call out to his mother, but at the same time, he was almost paralyzed with fear. The need to do something overwhelmed him and he quickly made his way to Charlotte's room.

"Mama," he whispered, shaking her furiously. "The intruder is in the kitchen."

Charlottes who had been nodding off, sat up. "What's wrong, Baby?"

"The intruder is in the kitchen," Sonny repeated, his heart pounding. "How do you know?"

"We gotta do something," He pulled at her arm. Finally realizing the urgency, Charlotte swung her legs onto the floor, pushed her feet into her slippers, and tiptoed to the kitchen door and pressing her ear against it, she listened. Sure enough, she heard the sound of the refrigerator door opening. Anger supplanted her fear. She looked around for something she could use as a weapon. Spying a curtain rod leaning against the window, the one she'd planned to replace one day when she had time, she picked it up.

"You stay here," she ordered, and opened the door. Fearful and anxious for his mother's safety, Sonny made his way to the window, and climbed out. Feeling his way along the fire escape, he climbed the iron steps as quickly as he could up to Bobby's apartment window. Luckily, the window was opened a little. "Bobby," he yelled into the room. "Where are you?"

"Whatchu doing out there?" Bobby opened the window fully and helped his friend in. When his breathing had slowed a little, Sonny told Bobby the situation.

"What's the matter, Sonny?" Taking off her coat and tossing it on the arm chair, Bobby's mother rushed to his side and put her arms around him.

"What's going on here? Bobby, Sonny?" Joe Thompson stood in the doorway.

"The intruder is downstairs in Sonny's apartment!" Bobby said anxiously. "We gotta do something."

"Yes, please hurry, my mother…" Sonny started to say.

"Boys, go upstairs and get Mr. Washington. Don't worry, Sonny. I won't let anything happen to your mother." Bobby's father started out the door ahead of the boys.

"Joe, shouldn't you take something to defend yourself? He may be dangerous," Mrs. Thompson exclaimed. Mr. Thompson reached into the closet and picking up Bobby's baseball bat, he strode out the door and down the stairs. Bobby and Sonny ran up to the Washington's apartment and pounded on the door. After explaining the situation to Mr. Washington, they went about arousing their other neighbors. Before long, almost the entire building converged on Apartment 2C.

By the time Bobby and Sonny arrived, the situation was well in hand. There at the kitchen sat Charlotte and Larry Clayton, the intruder. Surrounding them were Mr. Thompson, Mr. Washington, and several of the other tenants. Sonny rushed to his mother's side.

"Mr. Clayton was just finishing his dinner," Charlotte said smiling. "Would you like more coffee?" She extended the pot over his cup.

"Thank you, Ma am, Just a little," He replied graciously. He sipped the hot liquid slowly.

"Buddy, you got some explaining to do," Mr. Thompson said.

"Yeah," Mr. Washington said. "You been breaking into our apartments and taking things what don't belong to you." The other tenants agreed loudly. "Somebody should call the police."

"Have him arrested!"

"Thief!"

"Wait," Mr. Thompson said. "Give him a chance to explain himself."

"What's there to explain? He broke into our homes and stole from us."

"What did he take from you, a chicken, a piece of cake, an old robe, a torn shirt? Is that enough to send a man to jail for?" Mr. Thompson looked around the hostile crowd gathered in Charlotte's small kitchen.

"What have you got to say for yourself?" Mr. Washington asked. "Before I hit you up side your head with this here bat."

His eyes filled with fear, sweat breaking out on his brow, Larry Clayton dropped his head to the table, "I'm sorry. When I got out of the army, I didn't have no where else to go. I been living in the streets. I passed this place a few times and one day I came in, explored the building and decided to stay."

"Where's your family? Don't you have a home?" Charlotte asked.

"No Ma'am. I don't have no family. 'cept my daughter and I ain't seen her since she was a baby. She's living down in Alabama, I expect, with her mother."

"Why ain't you got no job like decent folk?" Someone asked.

"I can't work. I got wounded while I was in Korea." Larry pointed to a scar on the top of his head. "I get bad headaches and sometimes I fall out."

As he spoke, Sonny felt himself being drawn to this stranger. He reached out and put his hand on his shoulder. Larry turned around and looked at him. Then he smiled up at Charlotte. "This here's your son? I heard him playing his music. He's got a good collection of jazz."

"We not talking about no record collection. What I want to know is what are we going to do about him?"

"Why don't we get him a bus ticket down south to where his daughter lives," Bobby spoke up from the back of the crowd. He pushed his way through to the table and stood beside Sonny and his mother. "We could take up a collection and buy him a bus ticket," he repeated.

"He needs treatment first," Charlotte said.

"Doesn't the army provide psikey…," Mrs. Mobley stumbled over the word. "You know what I'm talking about…when a person ain't right in the head."

"They do," Mr. Thompson said. "Mr. Clayton, do you have a doctor?"

Larry shook his head. "I was suppose to go but I just never got around to it."

"We'll have to look into it," Charlotte said. Bobby pulled Sonny away from the neighbors and both walked downstairs and sat down on the stoop.

"Well, that's that. No more intruder," Bobby was almost sorry the mystery was over.

"Wonder where he was staying in the building. We searched everywhere," Sonny said.

"We could ask him. Or…" Bobby's face lit up, "I bet it's somewhere on the roof. Someplace we didn't look." He started back into the building.

Sonny heard Bobby's footsteps reach the steps and begin to fade as he climbed.

He quickly jumped up; reaching for the wall, he began to retrace his steps.

"Hey," he called. "Wait for me."

978-0-595-37041-2
0-595-37041-1